I0602091

THE SUPREME PURSUER

DARKNESS OF THE HUNT

AND OTHER STORIES

The Supreme Pursuer: Darkness of the Hunt and Other Stories is a work of fiction. References to real people, events, establishments, organizations, or locales are intended only to provide the sense of authenticity and are use fictitiously. All other characters, all incidents, dialogue are drawn from the author's imagination and are not to be seen as real.

Copyright © 2019, 2020, 2021 by Ty'Ron W. C. Robinson II.

All rights reserved.

Also available in eBook.

Battle For Astolat is also available digitally exclusive on Kobo. Also available in *The Haunted City Collection* and *The Dark Titan Audio Experience* in audio-format.
The Haunted City One-Shot: Helper's Hand also available on darktitanentertainment.com.
The Beasts of The Unknown originally published in *The Book of The Elect*.
Travis Vail, Spirit-Seeker: First Sins originally published in *Tales of the Numinous*.

Published by Dark Titan Publishing. A division of Dark Titan Entertainment.

Dark Titan Universe, Dark Titan Extended, and EverWar Universe are branches of Dark Titan Entertainment.

Paperback ISBN: 978-1-7369944-7-4

eBook ISBN: 978-1-7369944-8-1

darktitanentertainment.com

WORKS BY TY'RON W. C. ROBINSON II

BOOKS/SHORT STORIES

DARK TITAN UNIVERSE SAGA

MAIN SERIES
Dark Titan Knights
The Resistance Protocol
Tales of the Scattered
Tales of the Numinous
Day of Octagon
Crossbreed
Heaven's Called
The Oranos Imperative

Forthcoming
Underworld
Magicks and Mysticism
The Resistance vs. The
Enforcement Order

SPIN-OFFS
In A Glass of Dawn: The Casebook of
Travis Vail
Maveth: Bloodsport
The Curse of The Mutant-Thing

Forthcoming
Trail of Vengeance
War of The Thunder Gods
Maveth vs. The Swordman

ONE-SHOTS
Maveth, The Death-Bringer
Mystery of The Mutant-Thing
Shade & Switchblade
Retribution of Cain
The Mythologists
Ambush Bot
Kang-Zhu

COLLECTIONS
Dark Titan Omnibus: Volume 1
Dark Titan Omnibus: Volume 2
Dark Titan One-Shot Collection

THE HAUNTED CITY SAGA
The Legendary Warslinger: The Haunted City I
Battle of Astolat: A Haunted City Prequel (KOBO Exclusive)
Redemption of the Lost: The Haunted City II
Consequences of the Suffering: The Haunted City III (Forthcoming)

SYMBOLUM VENATORES
Symbolum Venatores: The Gabriel Kane Collection
Hod: A Symbolum Venatores Book
Symbolum Venatores: War of The Two Kingdoms
Symbolum Venatores: Elrad's Chronicles
Symbolum Venatores: Mystery of the Magician (Forthcoming)
Symbolum Venatores: Twilight of the Gods (Forthcoming)

EVERWAR UNIVERSE
EverWar Universe: Knights & Lords
EverWar Universe: The Damned Ones (Forthcoming)

PRODIGIOUS WORLDS
Mark Porter of Argoron
Raiders of Vanok (Forthcoming)
Praxus of Lithonia (Forthcoming)

FRIGHTENED! SERIES
Frightened!: The Beginning
Frightened!: The Light Sky (Forthcoming)

INSTINCTS SERIES
Lost in Shadows: Remastered
Instincts: Point Hope (Forthcoming)
Shadow in the Mirror: Instincts II (Forthcoming)

CHEVAH MYTHOS
The Eleventh Hour; A Chevah Mythos Story

THE HORDE TRILOGY
The Horde
The Dreaded Ones (Forthcoming)
Our Sealed Fate (Forthcoming)

DARK TITAN'S THE DEAD DAYS
Accounts of The Dead Days
Brand New Day: The Dead Days I (Forthcoming)

OTHER BOOKS
The Book of The Elect
The Extended Age Omnibus
The Supreme Pursuer: Darkness of the Hunt
Massacre in the Dusk (Forthcoming)

THE DARK TITAN AUDIO EXPERIENCE PODCAST
Season 1: Introductions
Season 2: In a Glass of Dawn
Season 2.5: Accounts of The Dead Days
Season 3: Battle For Astolat
Season 4: Hallow Sword: Cursed

THE SUPREME PURSUER

DARKNESS OF THE HUNT

AND OTHER STORIES

TY'RON W. C. ROBINSON II

CONTENTS

IN THE BEGINNING

A pair of scientists drove out into the Black Rock Desert after a notice of a meteorite had streaked over the skies of Nevada. Rallying those who caught a glimpse of its flight to contact the media. Therefore, this peculiar group of scientists had discovered the crash site and headed out into the desert on an early morning. Upon their arrival, they saw the burning surroundings smothered through the dirt and in the center was a crater. One scientist stepped forward, wearing a white hazmat suit as did the other two. He measured the crater, coming to the conclusion of twenty-feet wide and four feet deep. Grabbing their gear, they stepped own into the cater and what they had seen was an object. Appearing like an orb and seemly made of metal. The height of the orb on the ground was near above the knees of the scientists. Chromed and darker than onyx. The first scientist pulled out a metal pen and tapped the orb, there was no sound. Impressing them as they brought out their metal detectors to search the surroundings of the ob. However, they were amazed to learn their detectors were unable to scan the object itself.

"This is no ordinary metal." One scientist said.

"What do you think it is?"

"Not sure."

The second scientist went ahead, trying to scan the orb. Nothing on the detector. The third scientist took out a metal screw and tossed it to the ground. The second scientist waved the detector over the screw, and it beeped. Throwing the scientists off from their own knowledge of metals, they continued to search the surroundings of the object, the third scientist caught the sound of something scurrying around behind them above ground. He stood up and went to take a look.

"Found something?"

"Heard something."

"Like what? There's no one else out here. Or anything."

"Yeah. We haven't seen an animal since we drove out here."

"You think the crash spooked them? Scared them away?"

"Highly possible. Whatever this metal is, it could be lethal. Poisonous if touched."

"Now I see why we were commanded to wear these suits."

"The more you know."

The first scientist continued walking back up to the ground from the crater. Once he reached the top, he looked around. Nothing was in his sight except for the mountains and the sandy region of the Black Rock Range. One of the other scientists looked back, glaring up, seeing him standing and looking outward. His attention drew him from the work. The third scientist didn't bother to raise his head to get a glance.

"What is it?"

"Uh, it's nothing. Thought I heard something."

"Out here in the middle of nowhere?"

"Yeah. Sounds crazy, I know."

"Anyway, let's see what we can take back to headquarters."

They each went around the orb. Wiping the dirt from the hands as they reached down to grab the orb. Grabbing a hold of it and raising it from the dirt. They held it together as they proceeded to walk back up to the ground toward the van. Taking slow steps and using their own weight to move the orb upward. Reaching the van, they place the orb inside, covering it with plastic to avoid contamination. The first scientist shut the van doors as they heard the sound of dirt kick up behind them near the crater.

"You heard that?"

'I did."

"Told you there was something out here."

"Can't be."

"Then explain the dirt kicking itself up?"

"Tremor effect."

"Tremor effect? From what tremor? We didn't feel a thing."

"Understood. Let's just take this back to headquarters before they send the Guards to pick us up."

Getting themselves ready to enter the van, the dirt kicked up again. The scientists turned back, catching the dirt in the air before it vanished. The first scientist pointed.

"Explain that."

"Maybe it's a nearby volcano."

"Volcano? Last we checked, there aren't any volcanoes out here."

"Then what did that?"

The second scientist approached the ground where the dirt had raised and he knelt down. Wiping the ground and searching the dirt. He sighed, standing up and facing the other scientists. He waved his hands and shrugged his shoulders.

"It's nothing."

Walking back to the van, yet, he was stopped in his steps without notice. Trying to make himself walk and he couldn't move. The two scientists called for him to return to the van. Only to receive no response. Stepping out from the van and looking ahead, they both saw the second scientist frozen in place. Almost as if he was in a form of shock.

"Come on!"

The scientist did not move, yet, they could hear the fainting breaths exhaling from under his hazmat mask. The third scientist went to walk forward, only stopped by the first scientist.

"Something's wrong."

"What do you mean?"

"Something's out here. Like I've said."

"We have to help him."

The third scientist ran over to help his college and he reached for his hand. Trying to raise his hand, just to feel a flow of electricity moving through his body as his arm twitched as it rose up toward his colleague. He grabbed his arm and the third scientist noticed blood pouring from the hazmat suit. The sunlight glistened over him and what he saw were lens flares resembling blades piercing through the suit. He panicked and tried to back up from the scientist, only for his hand to be locked in with the scientists. He struggled to pull himself free from the scientist's hand, which began to weigh down on him as a cinderblock.

"I need help!"

The first scientist looked over, seeing the other scientist panicking as he tried to free himself from the third scientist's hand. Believing them to be joking, he didn't bother with them. Only yelling for them to return to the van. Meanwhile, as the scientist continued to panic, the transparent blades pierced through the scientist into the other. His panicked screams ceased and there was only a sense of quietness in the air. The first scientist looked out from the van and approached them both. Placing his hands on the scientist's shoulder, only for their bodies to collapse on the ground. Stumbling in his steps, he ran back toward the van, only to run into an invisible object. He struggled to breathe as he felt sharp pain flowing through is body. Slowly glancing down to his chest, he saw the blood pouring and the glistening reflections from a transparent force. The faint sounds of breath exhaled from his mouth and onto the invisible force, which slowly revealed itself to him. The smell of the air had quickly turned from smoldering dirt to burning metal with the scientist's eyes widen as he saw the invisible force in full before it decapitated him.

THE RALLY CALL

The U.S. Officials had later received word of the three scientists having gone missing. Therefore, they sent out a secondary unit to recover the orb and trace anything which may link back to the scientists. When the second unit arrived at the crater site, they recognized fabrics shredded on the ground, some covered in sand with dried blood sprinkled throughout the area of the crater. The unit returned to the base and detailed their findings. To which, the Officials had decided to call in a special ops unit.

"Send them in." The official said to the security.

Opening the doors, the unit entered and stood before the official. He measured them and nodded slightly as the security exited the room.

"Please sit."

The unit took note as they made themselves comfortable as possible in the room. The Official reached over to the side of his desk, grabbing a file. He opened it slightly to take a peek before passing it over to the unit's leader.

"You must be Adem Kabaar."

"I am, sir."

"And this is your unit?"

"It is."

"Before you open that folder, tell me. Everything I've heard about you guys, it's all true?"

"Every bit of it."

"And you guys are capable of accomplishing such a task as the one I'm presenting to you today?"

"Yes sir."

"Their names, according to what I've read are Brock, David, Scott, Brett, Austin, Escobar, and Miguel."

"That's their names."

Adem's unit was a mixed multitude of not only characteristics, but skill set and motives. Brock was the silent, yet deadly type while David was the charismatic soldier who sought out to charm anyone he may come into contact with. Scott was the determined soldier, willing to complete the mission at any cost. If it even caused him his life. Brett was the sharpshooter of the unit. Skilled with every weapon known to his service as a soldier. Austin was the speedster of the unit. His quick movements made all those they've fought move with second thought. Escobar deemed himself the comedic one of the unit. Making everyone laugh including the enemies. Miguel is the tracker of the unit. Able to spot the targets up ahead for several feet. His eyes were always spot-on.

The official nodded, permitting Adem to open the folder. Opening it, he read the details inside and was amazed. His comrades took glances into the folder and were astonished. Adem nodded and shut the folder, placing it on the desk.

"Is it all true?" Adem asked.

"Every word. So, are you and your team capable of completing this mission on your own?"

"Yes sir. We can."

"Very well. You're on. Head out into the desert and see what you can find. This object, is particularly important to the government and our country."

"I understand, sir."

SEARCH OUT OR BE SEARCHED

Adem and his unit made their travels out into the Black Rock Desert. Going on every track as the scientists had done. Their weapons were ready for a fight in case any opposing foes may show themselves. It was known among the ranks of Adem's unit being a target for mercenaries or militia groups. Making their way around the desert and up ahead, Miguel looked.

"The crater."

"You see it?" Adem asked.

"That's it up ahead."

Adem drove up toward the crater, stopping it once they had reached the van. The unit stepped out, scouting the surroundings. The area was silent with only a little whistle of wind. Adem walked toward the crater, looking down.

"There's nothing there."

"What do you mean?" Miguel asked.

"Whatever they were looking for. It's not here."

"So, we're just supposed to return back to base empty-handed?" Brett questioned.

"No. We keep searching. Whatever happened couldn't have gotten far."

"Hopefully, we'll get something extra out of this." Escobar noted. "Better be worth the prize."

"It's not like we're getting anything out of this." Austin answered. "Don't get caught up in some fantasy."

"A fantasy? Brother, this is an opportunity for all of us. Whatever it is they want, it must be worth something."

"Never mind that." Adem interrupted. "Right now, let's focus on finding whatever it is they came for."

Escobar scoffed and nodded as he went searching around the crater. Miguel approached Adem as they began walking down into the crater, seeing torn fragments laying in the dirt. Miguel knelt down, picking up a fragment.

"What is it?" Adem asked.

"Same material as those hazmat suits."

"Something must've happened out here I'm not sure exactly what."

"Well, looking at this fabric, only tells me one of their suits was damaged. By what? I'm not certain at the moment. Need to find more."

"Scott." Adem said. "Find anything in your area?"

Scott moved around an area not far from the crater. Yet, standing about seven feet from their location, he scouted the grounds for footprints of any kind. Scott looked around at the dirt, seeing nothing that caught his eye. He shook his head.

"No sir. Nothing. Not even kicked up signs of dirt."

Austin and David searched the van. Finding nothing inside besides tools and the strange fact the keys were still inside. Calling Adem over as he made his round, he saw the keys inside the van and the tools. David scoffed, wiping the sweat from his forehead.

"Where do you think the nerds ran off to?"

"They wouldn't have run on foot. The van is here. Something happened."

"What do you think took place?" Austin asked. "I mean whatever the Office wants, seems it's not here."

"You're right. It isn't here."

Adem shook his head and sighed.

"Oh well. Let's return to base. Inform them of our findings."

9

ARE WE ALONE?

Traveling through the desert on their way back to headquarters, the unit spoke of the crater and their theories as to what it may have been. Discussing flying saucers, returning dinosaurs, the coming of the Nephilim, and much more. They laughed concerning their theories while still taking them in a serious manner. Adem kept quiet as they moved through the desert, overhearing their conversation. In the distance, Adem caught the glint of a light and he leaned closer to see, revealing several figures.

"We've got company!"

The unit came to attention, seeing what Adem was staring at. Heading toward them were over a dozen militia men in three jeeps. They moved with speed toward them as the militia men began putting themselves out in the open, taking fire toward Adem's unit. He moved the vehicle to dodge to coming shots as Miguel returned fire. Austin looked around, seeing the desert only near them. Up ahead were a set of mountains. He pointed toward them and Adem turned toward them, leading to a chase with the militia behind them. Yelling and screaming while firing.

"The hell did these guys come from?" Miguel asked.

"Probably scavengers of equipment." Austin said. "Maybe they know what happened to the scientists."

"We don't have the time to ask questions." Adem said. "Besides, they'll kill us before we even give out a word."

The vehicles swerved through the dirt. Shots fired across from one another as two of the militia jeeps moved and drove beside Adem's. finding themselves cornered, Adem commanded for his unit to fire on both sides. The unit bolted from the door windows with ARs and machine guns, firing nonstop toward the two neighboring jeeps. The third jeep which was behind quickly came to a stop as the two jeeps on the sides began moving out of control from the gunfire. Escobar cheered as he fired his machine gun toward the driver of the jeep, causing the vehicle to flip into the air and crashed into the desert dirt. Adem looked through the mirror, seeing the third jeep making a U-turn, fleeing the desert. He grinned while shaking his head toward their arrogance.

"That's how we show them!" Escobar yelled.

"Nice one." Miguel replied.

"Alright then." Adem said. "Let's head back to base."

Riding out from the area back to the base, Adem caught a glimpse of something shining in the desert. Unable to make out the figure, the glistening flashed three times before vanishing into the nearby mountain. Unsure what to make of it, Adem kept the scene to himself and his mind was still as he heard his unit cheering on their victory.

WE ARE BEING WATCHED

Returning to base, Adem and his unit entered the office of the Official, waiting patiently for the Official's arrival. They sat and continued to wait while talking amongst themselves concerning the militia in the desert and the crater. Within minutes, the Official had arrived and only called for Adem to enter the office to discuss the mission. Adem followed and sat down before the Official.

"Tell me what you and your unit have found?"

"Nothing, sir."

"Nothing? What do you mean by nothing?"

"The object you sent us to retrieve was not there. Nor were the scientists."

"Shit. Then, tell me you found something. Anything at least."

"One of my guys found fragments from the scientists' suits. Shredded with drops of blood on them."

"Damn it."

"Their van was also there. Empty. It seemed like they were attacked by something. Whatever it was, we were unable to locate it."

"And the meteor is still out there." The Official said. "Who in the hell could've gone out there before we did?"

"We ran into a militia group while making our return here, sir."

"Militia group? What happened to them?"

"We took care of them."

"Ah. Good. Good. Perhaps, they have the meteor?"

"It's possible. My unit and I will go back out there at first light and track down the militia's camp. See if they have the object."

"Whoa. Hold on, soldier. First light?"

"Yes sir. It's night out. I'm unsure as to what we may face if we head out there in the dark. Especially in the desert."

"Adem, I'm not sure you understand the importance of such an object. This meteor, we must get out hands on it before anyone else does. Now, the fact that its missing is already an issue we cannot tolerate."

A knock sounded from the door. The Official called them in and inside walked another soldier, wearing all black with a cap. He handed the Official a tablet. The Official looked and his eyes widen. Adem could only look on, seeing a smile forming on the Official's face.

"Thank you." The Official said to the soldier before he exited the office.

"Ah. Good news. Finally."

"I'm sorry, sir?" Adem said.

"We've received an energy signature from the meteor. It's somewhere around Calico Hills. You and your unit will head out there immediately and retrieve it. At any cost."

"At night?" Adem asked.

"Yes sir. Your orders stand. I suspect you'll see them through."

Adem nodded slowly. Taking in the pressure as he stood up and exited the office. Outside, his unit stood up from their seats and approached him. Asking what he was informed. Adem told them their next mission. Brett looked concerned.

"Right now? At night?"

"Yes. Seems like we have no other choice."

Miguel nodded, taking in the order. Adem nodded back as the unit headed out and prepared themselves. Restocking their equipment before heading back into the desert in the darkness of the night. Questioning the mission's current stance, Adem informs the unit of their travel to Calico Hills to retrieve the object. Adem continued to speak and inform them of the object's true nature. A meteor which crashed the night prior.

"Is it alien?" Austin asked.

"They're not sure." Adem answered. "But, they seriously want us to retrieve the meteor. By any means."

"Then, it's of alien origin." Escobar said. "That's the only solution. We find it before the alien finds it."

"We'll see once we get there." Brett said. "Anyhow, who's waiting for us around Calico Hills?"

"Guess we'll find out when we arrive." Adem said. "That's all I know."

Riding out in the darkness, a light imbued itself above their vehicle. Uncertain as to what the light is emitting from. A helicopter? A plane? A balloon? Escobar went to take a look and what he saw was a very, very large object. Unsure what to make of it, he asked for binoculars to have a better look. Grabbing them from Scott, Escobar looked and what he was starting at was a ship. The ship's size was twice as large as a fighter jet and it emitted no sound. As if it had no engine. David was impressed, never seeing such a craft before. Brock on the other hand was concerned for their well-being.

"Well, I'll be go-to-hell." Brock said.

"It's a ship!" Escobar yelled.

"A what?" Miguel asked.

"A spaceship! Aliens, man! Aliens!"

Adem pressed the gear and moved faster to escape the light of the hovering ship. Once, the light had gone from the car, the ship moved faster, chasing the vehicle. The unit was uncertain as to make out the source of the ship while Escobar continued to yell out aliens. Adem suggested they continue to move through the desert to avoid the ship's light and they rode through the desert in the darkness. The ship followed them continually without any sense of delay. Passing through the mountains, the ship dodged the structures and twirled in the air to make its move. Adem looked at the mirror, seeing the ship behind them, hovering just several feet above them.

"We need to get rid of that damn thing." Miguel said.

"I know." Adem replied. "I know."

MEETING THE UNSEEN

Adem continued to move with haste as the object flew over them. Its light still tracking them down in the darkness of the desert. Escobar grabbed his AR from the floor and aimed it outside the window. Adem looked back, hearing the click from the gun. Escobar held himself steady on the car door, aiming upward toward the object, which flew only several feet behind them.

"What are you thinking of doing?" Adem asked.

"I'm going to take the shot!"

"You don't know if the object is bulletproof!" Brett yelled.

"Only way to find out is by taking the shot!"

Escobar fired a round, hitting the ship and the bullet didn't even make a dent nor a sound of impact. The ship continued chasing them and from the front of the ship, opened several slots. Within them were cylinder-pointed darts. The ship roared, letting out its first sign of sound as the darts bolted from the ship to the dirt. Escobar yelled, jumping back into the car as the darts plunged themselves into the ground. From Miguel's rate of eyesight, he perceived the darts to have dove nearly four feet into the soil. Adem turned toward him, seeing Miguel only shaking his head, suggesting he move much faster to get them to Calico Hills before the ship fires one of those darts onto the vehicle. Adem agreed as the rest of the unit began firing back toward the ship. The bullets fall to the ground as they collide with the ship's metallic texture. Still going, Adem looked ahead in their direction, noticing they're approaching Calico Hills. Informing the unit of their arrival, the ship unloaded with a blast of its own, crashing into the vehicle and flipping it over. Through the cloudy smoke in the night, Adem exited the vehicle alongside his comrades. Scratches and blood over their clothes. Scott shrugged it off as the ship hovered above them in such a stillness. They grabbed whatever firearm they could and aimed it toward the ship. Within seconds, the ship took off in such a speed unknown to them.

"The hell was that?" Miguel asked.

"You saw it too." Escobar said. "That's good. I was wondering if I was the only one."

Looking outward, Adem spotted the ship near the mountains. Miguel also saw it, pointing it out for the others to see through the darkness. Easy to be spotted due to the bright light emitting from the bottom of the ship. It made its landing atop the mountain and from there, a door had emerged, and something walked out. Something they were unable to see with their natural eyes. They gathered any supplies which remained as the vehicle was too damaged to travel. From there, they set up camp as they could hear the Gusher nearby. Adem sighed, looking up at the stars.

"What are we going to do now?" Miguel asked.

"Well, I guess we'll have to wait it out till morning."

"And what of that ship? Whatever came out of it is heading towards us. Means we're about to enter a battle."

"With something not of this world." Adem smirked. "Yeah. I guess we'll have to."

"What are we about to do?" Austin asked.

Adem nodded.

"Whatever that thing is out there. Shooting at us. It means it wants something. Most likely whatever had crashed into the crater last night. So, that means it's coming for us. This is a fight. A battle for our lives and potentially the lives of many others. So, yeah. This night we fight. By dawn, let's hope we make it home."

Brett nodded. Scott nodded. Austin nodded.

The team sat together and prepared for the coming force of the unseen figure. within the mountains near their campsite, the shadow figure emerged. Scouting the area and keeping close eyes on the unit. It moved through the darkness with ease. Like lightning, releasing the small sound of a hummingbird mixed with a jolt of thunder.

A FIGHT TO THE DEATH

Adem checked his watch, seeing it was only three hours before daybreak. The unit was prepared and geared up. They each set up positions and waited to see if the figure which arose from the parked ship would be coming. They waited for over thirty minutes, calmly waiting. Brock sighed and stood up from his post, going to take a piss. While he walked, he stepped on something. Looking down, he saw it to be something metallic due to the moonlight's glint. He rose his foot up and the metallic object exploded, grabbing the attention of Adem and his unit. They rushed over to the spot, only dinging the body parts of Brock scattered across the desert.

"Oh shit!" Escobar yelled. "Oh shit!"

"It's here." Miguel said, looking at Adem.

"Yeah. It's here alright."

Footsteps echoed from around them. Nearby at every corner. The unit banded together with their firearms aimed. They stood together hearing the unseen footers round them. The footsteps increased before more rapid. Adem and Miguel could sense the figure's movements. Feeling the wind blowing across their faces as they could hear the distant humming following the footsteps. David took several shots out, attempting to hit the invisible object. After the last round exited, the footsteps increased and rushed David. He gulped, sensing a sharp pain in his abdomen. When he gazed down, he saw a large blade sticking through his stomach. The blade exited with force as David fell to the ground, bleeding out. Escobar screamed and let out his rage with a continuing fire. In the darkness, Adem watched and what he managed to catch was a silhouetted figure shrouded in the darkness. It moved with such speed, the bullets were incapable of reaching. Adem screamed for Escobar to move, and he jumped across as the shadowed figure made itself known with a blade emitting from its wrist. The unit saw the figure in the darkness as it stared at them. The shadow paused itself, reaching toward its waist. Adem saw its movements and perceived it to have pressed something. The shadow covering the figure evaporated as it unveiled its true form to the unit.

"The fuck is that?!" Escobar yelled.

The being stood over seven feet and roared toward them. Covered in armor from head to toe. Its helmet resembling the samurais of Feudal Japan with the exception of its darkly glowing yellow eyes. The Pursuer is revealed. Standing firm with its hands up, the Pursuer chose to face them all in a fist fight. Escobar chuckled, seeing the Pursuer's stance.

"Is it doing what I think it's doing?"

"Don't play around." Miguel said. "This thing is not something to joke about."

Brett, Scott, and Austin held their rifles up and laid them down on the dirt. They cracked their knuckles, taking their steps toward the Pursuer. Adem looked at them with Miguel. Trying to reason with the three men. No word was taken in. they each agreed to fight to the death against the Pursuer and they rushed the figure. Giving it blows to the head, abdomen, and legs. The figure went down on one knee as Scott rushed over and kneed the creature in the head, cracking the helmet. Brett delivered several jabs to the back of the figure, finding its weak spot as he could see the skin peeking through the armor. Austin only stomped the figure in its sides. Escobar jumped as it entered the fight, punching and kicking the figure. Miguel took a step forward, but Adem stopped him. Unsure as to why, Adem wanted to see what the figure would do in order to retaliate.

"This thing's not that tough." Escobar said.

The Pursuer snatched Escobar's left leg by his ankle and pulled him under the beating and slipped itself out. Now, the unit was bashing down on Escobar unintentionally as the Pursuer escaped and attacked them from all around. Miguel rushed into the battle and was knocked back by the Pursuer's swinging forearm. Adem went ahead and started firing shots, hitting the helmet of the Pursuer. The unit was down and the Pursuer turned toward Adem, staring him down. Adem saw the glint on the armor and remembered what he saw hours before. He nodded slowly as he held the gun up.

"It was you. I saw you."

The Pursuer stood still, reaching toward its back and striking the ground with a metallic-like staff. The staff sparked with electricity and Adem stood calm, but within he was afraid. His gun was still aimed toward the Pursuer as Miguel rose up from the ground as did the others. Adem nodded toward them as they surrounded the Pursuer from all corners. The Pursuer roared, twirling the staff as the unit began firing rounds. The staff deflected the bullets as Adem held his gun steady, looking for an opening to hit the Pursuer directly. The Pursuer continued to deflect the bullets before striking Scott and Brett with the staff, tripping them to the dirt with shoving the staff in the chest of Miguel. Adem jolted and took the shot, hitting the Pursuer in the face with the round. The Pursuer paused and his hands went light, dropping the staff as it fell to the ground. Adem sighed while Scott approached the Pursuer, seeing that Adem's shot had made an impact, striking the Pursuer in the left eye.

"My man." Scott said. "You killed it."

"Killed it?" Adem questioned. "Are you certain?"

"You tell me. It's not moving. Check its pulse."

Adem knelt toward the Pursuer and went to check for its pulse. Unable to get a clear function, Adem hesitantly removed the helmet, unveiling the Pursuer's face. Seeing its dark-golden skin with little scaly features and sharp fangs. Its eyes were widened and enlarged. Much larger than with the helmet on.

"That's one ugly son of a bitch." Miguel said.

"Well, it's dead." Adem replied.

"Adem looked up, seeing the sun rising from behind the mountain as they could hear the Fly Gusher nearby in the distance.

"So, what do we do now?" Brett asked.

Adem remained silent, taking in the moment. A night he will surely remember. Several days later, the U.S. Government had retrieved the orb and the body of the Pursuer. All except for its helmet, which Adem chose to keep himself personally from the control of the authority. Adem placed the helmet inside his treasure room, keeping it there for a remembrance. However, inside the treasure room, the helmet began to glow and beep. A signal? Who's to know except for those of its kind.

A WALK WITH FEAR

Inside of an office. From the nameplate on the desk its the Mayor's office. The Mayor sat at his desk, sitting quietly as he was on a phone call.

"It would be a pleasure for you and your team to come investigate this."

Silence in the room as the Mayor listened on to the response.

"Thank you."

The mayor hung up the phone and looked out the window toward the small town.

People were walking through the small town going from place to place. Cars passed by, leaving the town and entering. Posted on nearly every building is a newspaper that depicts demonic activity happening at their local park. The paper advised no citizen of the town should enter the park until it has been cleared of its activities.

Inside of a lab were a set of five people. One stood by the board on the wall. The other four were sitting down at a desk. Together, they formed a paranormal investigation group comprised of Curtis, Sarah, Jim, and Izzie. The man standing at the board is their teacher in the supernatural, Professor Dan Simon.

"As you've been aware, I am sending you to a small town to investigate these demonic activities."

"You're not coming along with us, Professor?" Sarah asked.

"It depends on my schedule if I shall attend with you."

"If I may ask," Curtis said. "what kind of demonic activity are we dealing with?"

From the phone conversation, it seems that this is one of those usual demons that thrives on terrorizing uninformed people.

Jim shook his head after hearing Curtis' words.

"Isn't that like most of them we've encountered?"

"Pretty much." Izzie replied. "We can handle another demon. Send it back to his master."

Professor Simon glanced downward toward his watch.

"It's best that you all head out. The drive is only thirty minutes from here."

The group packed up their gear and exited the lab. Curtis was the last to leave, but Simon caught his attention.

"Curtis, make sure that everyone is prepared and ready."

"Yes sir."

Curtis had grabbed his bag and left the lab. Simon turned toward the board, continuing his work prior to the gathering.

The team arrived at the office with the small town's Mayor. Waiting for him to arrive, they spoke theories concerning the mystery as the Mayor walked in, seeing the young team. They stood up to greet him.

"You must be Simon's team of investigators. It's good to have you guys here."

"We're here to do our job of course."

"May we ask about these activities?" Sarah asked. "Occurring in your town's park?"

The Mayor went somewhat quiet before speaking as he closed the office door.

"We've never encountered anything like this before here. Never.

"Has anyone living here seen the entity that's causing these disturbances?" Jim questioned.

"There was one man who claimed to have seen some sort of demon, he called it. Said it was very tall and threatening."

Curtis nodded while Jim laid back in the chair.

"Anything else that we should know about, sir?" Izzie asked.

"That's about as much as we know here. No one's been in the park since. We've kept it locked down for all intents of purposes."

"There haven't been any fools to try and enter the park for their own game?" Curtis wondered.

"No. We have watchers patrolling the park 24/7."

Curtis stood up from his seat. The Mayor also stood up as the rest of the group followed.

"Well, Mr. Mayor, we'll do what we can about it and hopefully, these activities will cease permanently."

"Thank you all for coming and I wish you the very best of luck."

They shook hands and left the Mayor's office.

While they were outside, they proceeded to grab their equipment from the car. Curtis had gazed his sights over toward the park, which was only a few walks from where they're parked. Curtis notices a dark shadow moving through the trees of the park.

"We don't have to wait till the night." Curtis said.

"What makes you say that?" Jim asked with curiosity.

Curtis pointed toward the park. The team looked and turned back to Curtis.

"Because whatever is around there, it isn't waiting till dark either."

Curtis began walking toward the park. The team went ahead and followed him as they grabbed the last of their equipment. They entered the park, starting their investigation as the small town's citizens begin to come out of the buildings and watch them from the exterior of the park, being blocked by the patrolmen. Jim looked back, seeing the emerging crowd.

"Seems the spectators have come to watch us work."

"Let them watch." Izzie said. "They could learn something from this."

Using their equipment through the park itself, they begin to notice a strange mist rising from within the park itself. A dense fog also appears and begins to swallow up the park and the group. Curtis stepped forward.

"Stay where you are. Do not move until this fog has passed over."

"You're positive about that, Curtis?" Jim asked.

"I am. Once it passes over, we can regroup."

"Got you." Sarah replied.

The fog is dense to where neither member can see the other. All four are left on their own in the fog. They yell out to hear where the other is located in the fog. Calling names and places.

"Are any of you near me?" Curtis yelled.

"You sound distant." Sarah answered.

"I can't see you, man." Jim yelled.

"No kidding!" Izzie screamed.

Curtis continued to walk through the fog. Waving his hands through the thick mist, searching for a way out. Curtis continued until he felt something strange around him. Its presence was powerful enough to tremor Curtis. He paused himself and looked at his surroundings. Taking in a breath while being blinded by the bright mist, Curtis turned around and quickly found himself staring into the eyes of the demon.

"Damn."

Curtis was locked into eye contact with the demon. The demon looked to be a hybrid of man and demon. Its levitating off the ground and wearing a black cloak with scarlet and violet lining and a hood. Only its cold pale blue eyes and hands with long sharpened nails are visible. Its pointy ears can been seen from a close distant through its hood.

"What kind of demon are you?" Curtis asked.

"A different breed."

"Do you have a name? I've learned many demons and ghouls have names. I figured you have one as well."

"You may call me *Kamagrauto*. I have been waiting for the four of you to come here."

"You've known?"

"I knew before you made the trip. I knew before the phone call."

"How's that possible?"

In the distance, Curtis can hear the voices of the others calling out to him. He let out a yell of his own while Kamagrauto levitated silently.

"This way! Follow my voice!"

The group had come running through the fog. Reaching Curtis, they came to an immediate stop, nearly tripping from their own pace to find Curtis standing in the presence of Kamagrauto. The group was stunned and silent.

"Since none of you will speak, I will speak for you. I come from a realm not taught to pupils like yourselves. I've met people of your kind and entities higher than your kind. I've met men who have become great hunters and those who will become great hunters.

"You don't sound like some ordinary demon we've come across." Jim noticed. "What the hell are you?"

"I am not some ordinary demon. I am a lieutenant for the dark powers that live throughout these cosmos. I have been around since your kind's inception and I will be around at its end."

"Its end?" Sarah said. "You're telling us you know when humanity will cease to exist?"

"Again, I know many things. Things such as that will not come to your minds until its appointed time of course. There's still much for the four of you to learn."

"What gives you the right to come to this small town and frighten these people?" Curtis questioned.

"I didn't come here for those uninformed minds. I came here so that it would bring the four of you to me."

"The four of us?" Jim said. "For what reason? What purpose?"

"Yeah, I'm curious." Izzie said. "Why the hell us and not some other group?"

"Do not worry, I've done the same tactic to many in the past and I will continue so in the future."

The fog had begun to thin out. Kamagrauto spotted the dissolving very quickly. In a speed unnatural to the human eye.

"I will leave this place now and you can claim your glory from my disappearance. But, remember that we shall see each other again in the future days."

As the fog began to evaporate, Kamagrauto vanished from their sight. All that can be seen now is the group themselves as the people begin cheering.

The Mayor was also standing outside with the crowd. Once the mist had evaporated and the area was clear, he walked out into the field toward them as they exit the park.

"So, how did it go?"

"The demon is gone." Curtis answered. "The park is yours once again."

The Mayor shakes their hands as the town people thank them in mass. As if they've slewed a beast.

"We should get going now." Curtis told the group.

They returned to the lab later in the day. Speaking with Professor Simon about Kamagrauto and his eeriness. A demon unlike any other they've encountered. Even his voice caused them to quicken in their shoes. Simon listened closely to their words about Kamagrauto and his words toward them. Simon was quiet during their conversation.

"This demon knew you guys were coming into that town before I made the phone call?"

"That's what it told me." Curtis said.

"It also talked about the end of humanity and how it's been around since humanity began." Jim noted.

Simon rubbed his chin. Slightly concerned.

"I'm not sure what to make of it all."

"I will say, when this demon does return into the light, we will do what we can to get rid of it." Curtis proclaimed.

"How can we get rid of a lieutenant demon, Curtis?" Izzie questioned. "Because from what we could tell, he was much more powerful than some regular ol' demon."

Simon turned to Curtis. Eyes wide open.

"This demon was a lieutenant demon?"

"That's what it told us." Curtis said. "Said it takes orders from entities in higher places."

Simon sighed.

"I need some time to think on this. I will do more research into this as well. You guys go along now home and rest up."

They thanked him and left the lab. Only Curtis remained in the lab with Simon, walking toward him at the board.

"Professor."

"What is it, Curtis?

CURTIS

The demon also told us his name.

"His name." Simon said. "What was it?"

"He called himself Kamagrauto… and he walked with fear.

Simon stared at Curtis.

"I see. Very well. Go get some rest and we can talk about this tomorrow."

"Yes sir."

Curtis left the office. Simon took a breather as he walked over to his desk. Opening a drawer and taking out a book. The cover of the book appeared strange. Inscriptions carved into it from what seemed to be medieval-era art. He opened it and turned some pages. He came to a stopping point on a page which included the name Kamagrauto and a drawing of the demon himself with a description about its allegiance with an entity called *Dagor the Soul Eater*.

"This isn't looking good." Simon said with concern flowing from his words.

ONE MISSION: A SPY SHORT STORY

The sound of two gunshots echoed through the darkness. The end of the hallway was difficult to see through without some form of light. Coming through the dark was a figure. Human-shaped.. The figure continued to grow as it made each step forward.

Walking out of the dark area was a spy agent. Lean-figured, dressed in a casual suit with no tie. His focus was keen on the mission. The hallway in front of him had lit up with lights upon the walls and the rooms are closed. Silent and calm. Coming from around the corner into the hallway is Trevor moved through the hall with pace. He reaches the elevator and enters. Going up toward the eighth floor. The agent waited as the elevator made its move. The steady stop and as the doors slid open, the Agent saw two well-dressed men standing in the hall, guarding a room. The Agent has found what he's searching for. He backed up to avoid being spotted. He reached down toward his side, revealing his *Ruger LCP*. Raising it slowly, prepared to fire. Before he continued his act, he glanced over to the wall in front of him, seeing a fire alarm. He paused. Thinking. He moved swiftly, pulling down the alarm and setting it off through the hall.

"The hell?" One of the men said.

"What do we do now?" The second man questioned.

"We keep this door secured. Nothing else matters right now."

"You're sure the alarm won't trigger anyone to come up this floor?"

"For what reason would anyone come up here uninvited? They want to die early?"

From the other rooms on the floor bolted out hotel guests. Many of them. They make their way toward the stairs and the hallway is crowded. The Agent took a look, catching the hallway filled and the two men were still guarding the door. The guards themselves have their hand on their firearms for precaution. The Agent moved through the crowd without a misstep, placing a silencer over the muzzle to his Ruger. The Agent took the first shot before ducking down in midst of the crowd, The shot had killed one of the men as his body fell to the ground in the middle of the moving crowd. His partner turned over to look and noticed he wasn't standing on the other side.

"Where'd you go? We're on duty."

The Agent moved in closer as the hallway showed itself becoming empty. The Agent took the second shot, killing the second guard without fail. The Agent paused. He scouted the hallway, finding no one in sight besides the two dead guards. He nodded and opened the door. He walked into the room with his firearm in hand. Seeing it decorated with shelves of books, candles, and fancy décor. The Agent knew whomever had a room like this had the resources to acquire it. Discovering himself facing who's he come for. The target had been found. There was a man sitting at a desk, drinking a glass of scotch.

"Patrice O'Haire." The Agent said.

Patrice gestured his finger and from both side of the room emerged three more guards. Each with their firearms aimed at the Agent. The Agent glared toward each one of them, showing only an expression of a grin.

"If I only knew you were coming sooner I would've poured you a glass."

"Save yourself the favor. I'll drink after the mission is complete."

Patrice chuckled, laying back in the chair.

"You spies. You're all the same, you know. Always snooping

32

around in others' business. A bit nosy don't you think. Strangely enough, you always wonder why no one wants to take a moment and leave you guys be."

"I'm not here to chat."

"I know. I know." Patrice smiled. "Tell me please, why have you come to see me? What is it this time that has soured those on the opposite sides of the work?"

"You know what you've done." The Agent answered. "No need in repeating past words to rekindle your memory."

Patrice grunted.

"Again with this kind of talk. Do they teach you these words in your training. My goodness! All business and no fun."

"You forget the work of a spy. The mission is always the fun part."

"Sounds depressing." Patrice sighed. "Must be some kind of life, huh?"

"It has its benefits."

"Indeed." Patrice nodded.

Patrice signaled his guards to prepare to fire. The Agent knew the movements well, keeping his eyes locked on Patrice while watching closely the motion of the guards. Six to one. The Agent was confident in his abilities to succeed. Regardless of the numbers.

"Any last words, Patrice?"

"Just a few." Patrice said, turning over to the guards. "Take him."

The Agent gestured his eyes over to the opposite wall, noticing a fire extinguisher. He shot the extinguisher, shrouding the entire room in a fog. From there, he moved with silence throughout the room. The guards scattered themselves searching while Patrice remained at the desk, sitting down with concern.

"Shit!" Patrice yelled with a panic. "Find him! Kill him!"

The guards weren't able to see the Agent, yet he knew through the fog where the guards were placed. The scenery reminded him of target practice. From there, the Agent fired shots toward each of them without a single stop in his step. Only the sounds of thuds were heard through the white fog. Patrice couldn't see a thing, waving his hand in the air. The fog had cleared, Patrice found his desk surrounded by his guards, now dead on the floor, bleeding into the carpet. The Agent however, was standing in front of Patrice over the desk.

"I'm not going to repeat my last words."

Patrice jumped up from the chair, running out of the room toward the door to the hallway. The Agent followed him out.. Patrice made a move to the elevator, even though the fire alarm was still buzzing. The Agent watched as Patrice panicked at the elevator with fear. Patrice stood by the elevator, vigorously pressing the button and yet, the elevator doors do not open. Patrice took another look behind, seeing the Agent walking toward him. Patrice fell on his knees, looking down in terror. The Agent removed the silencer

"This was the only way." The Agent said.

The Agent fired the shot, shooting Patrice in the head. Afterwards, the Agent placed his gun into its holster and reached for his phone. He dialed a number. Someone had answered on the other end.

"The mission is done. I'm on my way."

The Agent hung up, leaving the body of Patrice on the floor. The fire alarm had silenced just as the Agent pressed the elevator button and the doors opened. Going down to the first floor. The Agent made his way outside the hotel. He walked toward a silver sports car parked near the entrance. Taking out the keys from his jacket pocket, he entered the car. Driving from the hotel. The Agent drove through the streets, not far out from him was the city of Vancouver. The Agent took a turn, making his way toward the city's airport.

NEW ORDER OF THE WORLD: AN EVERWAR UNIVERSE STORY

A corridor confined with metallic walls. Silent. Streams of white smoke emit from the steel-plated floors and ceiling. Down the hallway, the echoing sounds of tapping. The tapping morphed into beating and through the smoke a young man who is called Timothy. Dressed in all black with a long sleeve shirt and jeans. Wearing boots. Timothy is sweating and is running in the sight of fear. His life at the present moment is depending on his speed. Behind him we see four silhouettes after him. The silhouette later manifest into a guard. They're known as the Realm Guards. Soldiers of the City and loyal to their leader. Donned in black armored uniforms, carrying high-powered artillery firearms diverse from single ranges to plasma-ranges, weapons similar to the rainshockers of the Viper Realm. Their faces shrouded by their black masks and goggles. Resembling reapers. No emotion can be seen from them. They chase down Timothy through the corridor. Timothy keeps running and stops at a nearby room. He enters the room as quickly as he could run. Timothy took a small moment to catch his breath. Though, he can still hear the footsteps of the guards coming near the room. Timothy looked around and found himself in the presence of a robot. The robot is modeled after human structure, equipped with the A.I. from the technologies in the land. The name of the robot is A14-12.

"You appear to be in a rush."

"The Realm Guards are after me." Timothy said, catching his

breath. "I need to get rid of them."

"Now why would I assist you?"

"To keep them from killing me."

The robot examined Timothy and his garments.

"You're one of them."

Timothy nodded quickly. A14-12 recognized his intentions.

"Give me a moment."

Timothy waits for A14-12 to assist him, hearing the footsteps of the guards growing. Inching near him. Sweat drops from Timothy's forehead.

"They're coming closer!"

"Have some patience with me. After all, your kind know of patience."

A14-12 approaches Timothy with a device. The robot hands it to him. Timothy looks at it, unknown to what it is. He looks over at A14-12, questioning.

"What is this?" Timothy waved.

"If you want to evade the guards, hold it above your head."

Timothy scanned the device. Intrigued by its design.

"Is this some kind of teleporter?"

"No. They don't place them within this room. What you're holding will be good enough for your sudden cause."

The guards are near as their voices can be heard in the distance. Timothy holds the device above his head. A silver-colored mist fell from the device around him. Timothy notices himself becoming transparent. His flesh vanishing before his eyes. He knows he's becoming invisible. The guards burst into the room. Guns in hand. They circle the room, seeing only A14-12 standing. Calm demeanor for a robot. One guard approaches him. Eyes locked on tight.

"Mechroid, have you seen an enashian run past here?"

"I have not. You're the first I've seen this day."

"If you encounter the enashian, alert the Highguard."

"I will do that."

The guards leave the room and move further down the corridor. A14-12 looked around, scanning the room. Through the scanning process, the robot could see the invisible Timothy standing against the wall.

"Ah. There you are."

The robot grabbed a small firearm from the table and fired an electric bolt toward Timothy. The bolt hits Timothy in his left knee. He jolts and becomes visible again with the electric currents revealing himself.

"Why did you do that?!"

"You didn't make yourself visible, so I had to do it."

Timothy shook his head with a slight nod.

"Thanks."

Its not a problem. But, since you're here and finding your way out of this land. I assume you're on your way to finding the other renegades.

"The others?" Timothy jolted, waving his hands in disagreement. "No. No. I'm just trying to get out of this place with what I know."

"But, you're an enashian."

Timothy paused . The mechroid is aware Timothy isn't understanding the meaning of his words.

It's better of you to find them. You can lead them here to save the enashians and mechroids from the tyranny we live under.

"Why are you so interested in all of this?"

"I have my own reasons."

Timothy takes it in. Seeing what appears to be some form of character within the robot. A care perhaps? Unsure as to where the renegades may be.

"I'm on my way out of here anyway." Timothy let out a faint sigh. "I'll try to find the renegades."

"Maybe they'll find you."

"I'll take your word for it."

Timothy walks toward the door.

"We'll see once I get back. If I make it back."

"You'll be well." A14 said with certainty.

Timothy had left the room, running through the corridor and finding the exit. He exited the corridor and continued running.

Timothy runs outside of the base, he looks around, seeing himself surrounded by techno-buildings and flying drones made of beaten down metals. The buildings were as tall as skyscrapers and the air was lukewarm. The sounds of an electrical howling can be heard roaming in the skies above him. The city itself was one with great heaviness and astounding beauty. The structure looked to have been built many years ago. The aging itself had no greater effect than to instill fear. Its scent was of a burning fire mixed with electricity and a strange catch of cinnamon. He could hear the faint, yet squealing sounds of humans screaming coming from within the city. Their screams were of torment. It irked him, making his escape and finding himself entering the wilderness.

Timothy walks through the wilderness, known to those around the area as the Desolate. Nothing can be seen but a vast desert. Sand and rocks sit in places. Trees little to none. Few cactuses stood apart form each other. Scattered. Timothy walks through the Desolate as the wind slowly picks up and dust flies through the air. Timothy covers his face with his arm to avoid having sand fly into his eyes, nose, and mouth. He keeps walking as the wind increases in strength. The heat has increased in temperature and it begins to tire Timothy out. Yet, he continues moving through. After walking several more feet from his previous location, Timothy appears to spot a small structure up ahead.

"Is that a base?" Timothy glared.

As he goes to take another step, Timothy is stopped and lassoed from behind. Timothy looks down at the lasso around his torso. Hearing what is someone running toward him from behind, he turns his head, only to see a fist flying towards him. The fist punches Timothy, knocking him unconscious. Timothy awoke with a jolt. Beginning to regain his senses. Now knowing he's sitting down and his arms tied behind the chair. He's aware he's sitting in the middle of a room. The room is dark and the only light source he can see is coming from the sun above him through a circular hole in the ceiling. The room, of what Timothy could see was dirty with the Desolate sand. It smelled of vehicular oil and sweat. Its odor bothered Timothy, but he kept himself focused. Timothy tried looking around the room, seeing no one. He questions the scenario. He's tied up, so there must be someone within the room with him.

"OK." Timothy looked around. "This is strange. Anyone in here?"

No sound of a reply returns to him. Timothy quieted himself. Taking in a breath.

"Hello! Is there anyone in here besides me?! I'm pretty sure there is!

Footsteps are heard in front of Timothy. Though, he cannot see who's walking as they are shrouded in the thick darkness surrounding him. The footsteps come closer and more footsteps are heard. They are surrounding Timothy and he knows it. Shaking around in the chair to set himself free. A voice comes through the darkness facing him.

"No need for you to do such a thing." A voice echoed.

Timothy stops shaking and stares into the darkness. Looking for the location of the voice. Squinting his eyes.

"Who's there? Speak again."

The footsteps are heard once more. Only this time, Timothy can see the boots coming into the light and after several more steps, Timothy can see the one who spoke to him. A middle-aged man. Rugged in appearance, wearing cargo attire with a sleeveless shirt with scruffy facial hair and a almost shaved head. The man was the leader of the Renegades.

"Here I am."

Timothy looked. Seeing Castle in front of him. From all around Timothy and Castle enter into the light the other renegades. About a dozen of them.

"As you can see, you're not alone."

"Why am I tied to this chair?"

"Few of the watch guards caught you roaming through the Desolate, alone. They believed you to be a shell for the realm guards. You're not one of them are you?"

"I am not one of them." Timothy replied.

"Your uniform represents the Realm. Therefore, it makes you a loyal subject to the Dictator."

Timothy gazed down at his uniform. He even looked around, scanning the renegades' own attire. He knew they could tell the difference between the ones who are aligned with the Dictator and those who are the renegades. The apparel of the renegades were cargo pants and militaristic vests. Both dirty and wet from water.

"I see your reasoning, Mr.?"

"Just call me Castle. I would like to know your intent of running through the Desolate alone."

"I was told that I could find you out here. Maybe convince you to help free the others trapped in the City."

"Is that right?"

"It is." Timothy glared at the Renegades. "I can guess by your questioning that you're the leader.

"I am. Been leading the renegades ever since the fall of our freedom came to pass.

"I can see they trust you."

"Damn right they can. Most of them I been with me through the battles. Lost friends and loved ones along the way. Yet, together we stand tall."

Timothy nodded. Castle searched him, seeing if he could learn

Timothy's motives.

"Tell me why you're here? Honestly."

"I escaped the confines of the City and ran into the Desolate. That's how your watch guards spotted me. I was told to find renegades by a mechroid."

Castle looked intrigued. Crossing his arms.

"What kind of mechroid?"

"An espionage mechroid. Operated with the technology within the City."

"Did it have a name?"

"Yeah."

"Tell me its name."

"That's not important. I can attest to that."

Castle stared at Timothy. His arms steady. No movement and little emotion.

"Why?"

"Try me."

Timothy nodded.

"A14-12. That was its name."

Castle looked over at the other renegades. They turned and spoke to each other before Castle focused his attention back to Timothy. Timothy could see the seriousness in Castle's eyes. Castle bent down toward Timothy, looking him in the eyes. Timothy shook with a certain fear. Castle's presence was something to fear. Even some of the renegades feared him.

"Where is this mechroid now?"

"Still in the City."

Castle grinned.

"I'm not certain to take what you've told me as fact."

"It's all true. That's the only reason I'm in this chair right now!"

"The only question is how could we enter the City when it is guarded by their snipers?"

"I…" Timothy shook. "I know a way inside the City."

"No shit." Castle scoffed.

"What I meant to say is I can take you and your group to the City. Sneak into the city and we can free the others."

Castle shook his head. Timothy couldn't tell if he accepted or rejected what he had told him. Castle stood in front of Timothy and cocked his head.

"How can we trust you?

"You can trust me. I'm not a betrayer.

"We'll know eventually. But, right now, we'll make our move into the City. And you'll be leading us in."

Timothy jerked with haste. Rattling the chair.

"Me? I don't understand?"

I'm not giving you the opportunity of bringing myself and my soldiers into death."

Timothy paused himself.

"I see your reasoning.

"That's a good start."

Castle reaches on the side of his leg and pulls out a knife. Timothy stops moving as Castle takes the knife and cuts the ropes from Timothy and the chair. Timothy sighs with relief as he stands up slowly from the chair. Castle takes the knife and places it onto Timothy's throat. Timothy gulped.

"Because if you wrong us in any way. I will personally kill you. Do you understand?"

"I understand."

Castle smiled, placing the knife back into his pocket.

"Good to know."

Castle looks to the renegades. He nods with a smirk on his face. The renegades rally up and equip themselves with their weapons, ranging from energy guns, plasma grenades, knives, and energy-coated knives." Timothy sees them gathering their weapons. Feeling uneasy as he's just walking through the area.

Outside of the base, the renegades are sitting on dirt bikes, preparing to ride off toward the Realm's City. Timothy himself gets onto a bike. Castle sees him on the bike and points at him.

"You get in the front!" Castle pointed outward.

"You and your soldiers have the firepower." Timothy replied. "Why do I have to be in the front?"

"Get your ass in the front!"

Timothy went and sat atop the bike in front of them. Castle gave the renegades the command to follow.

The renegades had reached the city. They paused for a moment and Castle turns over to Timothy. Pointing at the city. Glancing up to the skyscraper structure and moving crafts.

"Lead us in."

"Of course. Follow along quietly. Hide your bikes over near the walls. The guards rarely do searches on this side of the city."

"Hide the bikes." Castle commanded the Renegades.

The renegades leave their bikes next to the wall. The wall is made up of a mixture between bricks and titanium wiring. The wiring glowed various colors with electricity flowing through it. It appears as if it was meant to be a twisted, yet somewhat beautiful sight to outsiders. Timothy guided Castle and the renegades toward the location where he had exited the city during his escape. The surroundings were clear as Timothy opened the door and they entered into the corridor.

Castle walked behind Timothy while the other renegades watched every corner. Prepared to fire.

"I have to ask you, kid. Why are you involved in all of this?"

"It's all a mistake." Timothy answered.

"A mistake? Saving others from tyranny is no mistake."

Timothy stops and faces Castle. Castle reads his eyes. He senses something within him. Hidden behind his outward visage.

"I see. You're a deserter."

Timothy took note and continued walking.

"You turned against the Realm and for good reason."

"I turned against them because of the destruction they plan to bring."

"They've always plotted destruction. It's nothing new."

"Be that as it may. It doesn't spare me from the death I will receive."

"Death is only a solution of theirs. To trigger fear. What you've done, whether it is out of cowardice or bravery, it's for a greater cause."

Timothy listened to Castle's words closely.

"Hope I don't screw it up."

"You won't. You've shown me enough to figure that."

Walking through the corridor slowly, Timothy returned to the room A14-12 was in. Timothy enters the room with a storming haste.

The electric room is the base for the City's primary grid system. The walls glowing with a bluish hue as the energy flows through the wiring. Timothy looks around the room, but A14-12 is nowhere to be seen. Castle enters the room and looks around. Seeing the amount of tech that sat within its walls.

Castle scanned the room entirely. His eyes keen to the doorways.

"Look at this stuff."

Timothy looked over toward Castle. Shaking his head. Castle doesn't understand what Timothy's problem is or what he's trying to say.

"What is it?"

"The mechroid isn't here."

"Maybe it went to help the others find a way out."

"Maybe."

Not finding the mechroid, Timothy led them outside of the electric room.

As they step out into the corridor, on the other end are realm guards. Staring down Timothy, Castle, and the renegades. Their energy guns are searing and buzzing. Prepared for fire.

"Well, I'll be damned. We have company."

One of the realm guards raised up his plasma-range.

"Renegades! You have one request. Surrender yourselves now and come with us to be questioned and judged."

Castle stood firm. Determined about his next move as were the Renegades.

"I'm not going anywhere with you."

"We will now respond in the proper circumstance."

Castle stood his ground with the renegades. The realm guards begin firing toward the renegades. They run across the corridor. Some enter the electric room. Castle fires back at the guards with the renegades. Flying energy blasts zooming across the corridor back and forth. Timothy ran out of the corridor and into another doorway, which led down into another corridor.

Timothy ran through the second corridor and as he reaches its end, he bumps into A14-12. Standing around the robot are humans, beaten and battered, looking to escape. Timothy smiled.

"Where were you earlier?"

"I was preparing to aid these people for escape."

"How would you get them out?"

"I knew you were coming back with the renegades."

"How?" Timothy asked.

"I have my ways."

Timothy nods and leads them out of the corridor and toward the exit. He opens the door and the people barge out of the corridor.

"Get away from this place as far as you can."

The people run outside and towards the Desolate. Timothy and A14 return to the first corridor, where they can hear the echoes of firing energy blasts. Nearing the doorway, the blasts slowly cease and turn into silence. Timothy, hesitant to open the door, opens it anyway. Timothy and A14 enter the first corridor and within the corridor are dead renegades and dead guards. They look and see Castle with several other renegades exit the electric room. Castle smiles and laughs as he approaches Timothy and A14.

"Where did you go?"

"I helped A14 set some humans free." Timothy looked around. "I see that you've managed to take them out."

"As you can see, I lost some of my own. Enough as I can manage at the moment."

Timothy turned to A14 as did Castle.

"We must leave this place now. She's coming."

"Who's coming?" Timothy wondered.

Castle shakes his head looking at Timothy as they proceed to exit the corridor and return to the outside.

"You mean to tell me that you don't know who "she" is?"

Timothy stood confused.

"I don't know who A14 is talking about. Who is this "she"?"

"We must hurry."

"Who is she?" Timothy asked.

They approach the exit door and open it. Running to the outside of the City.

Running outside, they find themselves chased by drones and several realm guards. Castle sees it and isn't happy about it. His face twists with anger and haste.

"Damn!" Castle yelled.

"This isn't good."

"You don't say."

A14 starts to beep as they get on the bikes. The mechroid can sense someone approaching them near the realm guards. A14 knows of that peculiar presence.

"Here she comes."

"I'm asking, who is she?"

Castle turned to face the guards. It was there he saw her in the distance. The footsteps sounded rough against the dirt. With vigor.

"Look ahead, kid." Castle pointed.

Timothy looks and see her. A woman dressed in all grey. Her dark hair down to her shoulders. Her eyes glowing of emerald. He lips red as blood. Her countenance as wicked as one could read. She is the Dictator.

They ride off into the Desolate as realm guards approach the Dictator. Bowing before her presence.

"Should we pursue them, my Lady?"

"No need." The Dictator grinned. "Everything is in proper order."

The realm guards returned to the City while the Dictator stared, watching the bikes ride out further into the Desolate.

BATTLE FOR ASTOLAT

A CONFLICT OF THE HAUNTED CITY

I

The city of Astolat stood tall amongst its neighboring regions. Astolat is the city of Elaine and her father, Bernard. The city was ravaged by an army. An unseen army, who appeared from the air. The Astolat army combated the strange and ghostly force. The ghostly army overtook the soldiers, killing them within an instant. Bernard took Elaine and they both went into hiding. Having no other choice, but to escape the city as the ghostly army sacked their home and their leader appeared before them. Dressed in a dark violet cloak with his face rarely seen, although his eyes appeared to reveal themselves. The eyes looked dead, but there was another force living through them.

Residing at a secondary home, far into the wilderness, away from Astolat. Elaine writes a letter, detailing the event of Astolat's invasion and sacking by the unknown force. Bernard entered the room, seeing her writing the letter. He's intrigued.

"What are you up to, my daughter?"

"I'm sending word for help."

"Help?"

"Yes. I know of some men who can aid us in taking back

Astolat."

"What kind of me are these that are capable of doing such a matter?"

"A set-apart kind." Elaine said. "They know justice."

She finished writing the letter. Walking outside toward the pigeon cage. Placing the letter, the bird flew in the air with Elaine watching. Bernard approached Elaine from the side, also seeing the pigeon flying away.

"Hope you're right on this cause."

The pigeon flew several miles, until it reached the city of Old Jerusalem. The city was the home base to the Warslingers of the Heptad. The pigeon reached the Temple of the Heptad. Sitting outside the temple was Joshua of Ephraim. The pigeon flew to him, landing in front of him. Joshua sees the rolled letter. He grabbed the letter and the pigeon flies off, returning to Elaine. Joshua entered the temple, seeing the other Warslingers.

"Brothers, this was just delivered to us." Joshua said, handing them the letter.

Moses The Leader grabbed the letter. He opened it and read. The Warslingers stood around him, waiting for him to speak. Moses read the letter to himself and rolled it back up. Nodding, he turned to his brethren.

"It appears we have work to do. First, we make way for Old Camelot. Inform Knight Arthur Pendragon of these details. He must come along with us. For he is also our brother in this walk."

"Moses." Joshua said. "What did the letter inform?"

"It informed of some danger that has been committed. Now, it is our task to rid this malevolency from this place."

The Warslingers make ready to travel to Old Camelot, leaving Old Jerusalem on horseback. In the matter of time, Elaine awaits an answer from the Warslingers as des her father, who worries for Astolat's remains. Believing the ghostly army will turn their city into rubble and ashes.

Entering Old Camelot, Knight Arthur Pendragon was there at the gate to greet his brothers-in-arms. Standing by his sides were Maiden Guinevere and Knight Lancelot. Moses stepped from his horse and walked towards the king of Old Camelot. Extending arms, the two hugged.

"Wasn't expecting to see you this soon." Arthur said.

"Wouldn't be here if it wasn't of importance."

"What's happened?"

"We can talk inside."

"Of course."

Walking inside the castle, they reached the Great Hall, where the Spherical Table sat. the Warslingers all sat at the table while Lancelot guarded the doors. Guinevere left their presence as they started to discuss their matters.

"Now, what's taken place?"

"We've received a letter of distress from the land of Astolat. It appears something has been ongoing in the land for a while and under our sight."

"Invasion from Old Egypt?"

"We won't know until we reach Astolat. We came because we'll need you with us."

Arthur nodded.

"I'll go along. Of course, being a Warslinger myself, it is my duty."

"Believe me, I can see you have plenty to deal with. Ruling a kingdom and being a Warslinger. Only few souls can achieve both titles and become a master at them."

"Speaking of such, how's Old Jerusalem?"

"Peaceful. *El* is there with us. Always."

Arthur nodded with a smile as they headed out of Old Camelot, traveling toward Astolat.

II

Making their entrance in Astolat, the common folk watched in awe and fear as the Warslingers came in on their horses. They made their presence known. Moses turned to Joshua, Daniel, Henrich, and Charlton as they settled their horses near the station.

"The four of you will remain here." Moses commanded. "Keep this place guarded and the people safe."

"Where are you heading?" Charlton asked.

"Myself, Noah, and Arthur will be speaking to King Bernard at their second estate. They refuse to return here until the task is done."

Moses, Noah, and Arthur rode off, leaving the other four Warslingers to settle into the city. They looked toward one another before going separate ways throughout the city, finding a spot and keeping guard. Due to the lack of protection from the Astolatians.

"They carry no weapons." Charlton observed.

"They leave the fighting to the soldiers." Daniel replied. "They don't join in on the battles."

"But, we're supposed to protect them?"

"I know it irks you, Darrain. But, just this once, don't let it bother you."

Far from Astolat, the three Warslingers arrived at the second estate. Seeing two Astolat Knights keeping guard. They approached the door and it opened with Elaine standing in their presence. She ran out and hugged each of them with tears in her eyes. Relieved they received the letter and took the call. Bernard stepped foot outside, seeing the Warslingers. He nodded with great respect.

"It's an honor to have you here, Moses."

"We'll do anything to rid your city of the malevolency which circles it. May we come in and discuss this?"

"Of course."

They entered the home, sitting at the table near the kitchen. Elaine brought them some hot tea, due to the wintry weather occurring. Bernard sat with them while Elaine stood back.

"Tell us what's been happening."

"They appeared out of nowhere." Bernard said. "They showed up and started ransacking the city. Killing some of the people."

"What did they look like?" Arthur asked. "Were they possible adversaries to Old Camelot?"

"No. They didn't seem to be from our world. Nor any of the Worlds."

"You're saying they possessed some mystical power?"

"They must have. To do the things they've done. Levitation, portal binding, teleportation. They had to have been very precise in their arts."

Moses nodded. He looked over to Noah, who also nodded.

'This sounds eerily familiar."

"Do tell." Arthur noted.

"Myself and Noah in the early days dealt with a small army which did such feats. This was when the Heptad was yet to be formed and the Warslingers were few in number. This was during the early stages of the Eastern World War. Those who didn't possess weapons of any kind chose magic as their arsenal. Some we trusted, turned on us, doing the same as Bernard spoke."

"So, will you help us in taking back our city?" Bernard asked.

"I must ask." Noah said. "We just came from your city and only the people are present. No signs of any threats."

"You mean they left?"

"Did they leave after the ambush?"

"Me and Elaine left before we could tell."

Moses stood up from the table. Noah and Arthur followed his movement. A Warslinger custom. Elaine walked to the table and Bernard stood up.

"We will aid you in finding the source of this mystic power. Once it is done, you may return to your city."

"Thank you." Elaine said.

"We're just doing what we must."

The Warslingers exited the home with Bernard behind them. As they sat atop their horses, Bernard approached them.

"You can stay here for the night. We have plenty of room."

"Much thanks is obliged." Moses said. "However, it is best we return to Astolat. To keep guard. We already have four Warslingers present. I will return to you once the job is done."

"I wish you the best." Elaine said.

"Take care of yourselves." Arthur said.

The Warslingers rode off.

Later in Astolat, the four Warslingers have received accommodations in the castle chambers. One to each of them. Henrich sat in his chamber, counting the hours. A knock came from the door, catching the young Warslinger's attention.

"Door's open." Henrich said.

The door opened and Charlton entered. He shut the door behind him and approached Henrich, sitting across from him at the table.

"What is it?" Henrich asked.

"You know me. You know how this all goes. What do you

think's happening here?"

"Some magic wielders probably causing a ruckus. We've dealt with such before."

"Indeed." Charlton nodded. "But, have you ever considered the cost of us doing the work of another? I mean, this King Bernard has knights of his own. Why are we here doing their bidding?"

"I'm not getting what you're speaking."

Charlton sighed.

"We're supposed to protect the ones from evil. Those who can't protect themselves."

"Yes."

"This city already has protection in the form of these knights. We're not needed here. For all *El* knows, we could be needed in Old Egypt or Old Rome."

"I get your point."

"Do you? Because from what I've seen today, you've been blindly obeying every command given."

"I'm not in authority, Charlton." Henrich proclaimed. "Neither are you. We all have our place in the Heptad. In *El*."

"Yes, we do." Charlton nodded in agreement.

He stood up and walked toward the door. Henrich watched him.

"Just remember." Charlton said. "Think about why we're here and not elsewhere. They're something going on and we need to be careful."

"I'll take your word for it." Henrich replied.

Charlton left the room and Henrich laid down on the bed, falling asleep.

Later in the night, Moses, Noah, and Arthur returned to the city and entered their own chambers. All the Warslingers were asleep for the night.

III

The following morning, the Warslingers gathered the Astolatian Knights to the court of the castle. Moses sat before them, giving them instructions on how to prepare for the returning army and the attacks in which will be operated. As Moses continued giving the instructions, a fellow soldier bolted through the doors, his face showing minor scars compared to his damaged armor.

"They're back!" The soldier yelled before falling on the floor.

The soldiers all stood up and ran outside. Moses and the Warslingers held back as the remaining soldiers left the room. Joshua took a step forward, yet stopped by Moses.

"We need to help them."

"And we will." Moses said. "Give it a second."

"A second?"

"This army doesn't know of our presence. Therefore, we have the alterative surprise."

Moses turned to the other Warslingers and nodded.

"You know what to do. Go now."

The Warslingers went their ways outside the castle. Moses walked on and Joshua followed him. Eventually heading outside to see the battle in front of the city and on the castle grounds. They saw the army clearly. Dark armor, scaly and sharp. Their faces covered by their burnt helmets. Moses recognized such a garment.

"This isn't new." Moses said.

"What do you mean, my Leader?" Joshua asked.

"I know who's leading them. And he's close."

The Warslingers appeared from their corners around the castle, catching the army off guard. Henrich and Charlton used their arkshooters, firing rounds in the heads and chests of the mystical soldiers. The rounds from the shooters piercing through their armor like a nail through a leaf. Daniel, Noah, and Arthur swiping through the battlefield. Arthur wielding *Excalibur* while Daniel held the *Faithsword* and Noah carried the *Arkaxe*. The army was quickly being defeated with the Astolat knights cheering on the skills and fighting styles of the Heptad. Through their cheering, Moses and Joshua stepped out into the field as Henrich fired another round at the mystic soldier. The battleground set still with only the cheers of the Astolat knights. The Warslingers came over, standing next to their leader.

"This is not over." Moses uttered.

"Then, where is their leader?" Charlton asked.

"Right there." Henrich said, pointing toward the east, near the entry point of the castle grounds.

Standing before them was indeed a man, covered in scaly armor. Appeared burned, but with a violet and reddish hue. His face was with a helmet, giving him the appearance of having six eyes with a hood and cloak. The Astolat knights attempted to rush him, however, he raised his arms, lifting them off the ground and tossing them across the grounds of Astolat. He was strong in the mystic arts. Moses stepped forward.

"I know him."

"You do?" Arthur said. "How?"

"Because, he was once one of us."

"*Mosheh*." The figure spoke. "We have met once more."

"Yes, we have, Azotus Vorr."

IV

Moses and Azotus stood facing each other. Moses held his staff tightly as the sapphire began to glow.

"It has been some time." Azotus said.

"Not long enough." Moses replied. "You're the leader of this army."

"I am. They came to me after our last encounter."

"Those who sided with you became endowed with mystical abilities?"

"As did I."

Azotus held his arm out and from the thin air appeared a staff. Similar to Moses' own, yet darker, burnt, and glowing wih a violet and reddish hue of energy. The staff was endowed with the same mystical power as Azotus.

"Why don't we settle this like warriors." Azotus said.

"So be it."

The two staves collided, giving off a shockwave of energy. From there, the Warslingers aided the remaining Astolat knights against Azotus' army. The entire area of Astolat was now a battleground with Moses and Azotus standing in the middle, staves colliding and blasting energy. Henrich and Charlton stayed together, firing rounds toward the soldiers.

"What about Moses?" Charlton asked.

"He can take care of himself." Henrich replied. "We need to deal with these soldiers."

The Warslingers take the fight to the soldiers, wiping them out with some of the Astolat knights finishing them off. Moses and Azotus continued their bout, with Moses swiping the staff against Azotus' chest, knocking him across the field. Azotus arose and slammed the ground with his staff, causing a minor tremor. Stumbling Moses.

"Never did like the ground quake." Azotus said.

Azotus rushed toward Moses with staff in hand. In came closer, yet, Moses turned to him with the sapphire staff facing him. Once Azotus was in touching distance, the staff emitted a bright flash of light. The light pushed Azotus from Moses and in doing so, the soldiers of Vorr vanished due to the light.

"What kind of power is this?" Azotus questioned.

"The power you walked away from." Moses replied. "Now, go and never return."

Azotus took steps forward, trying to breach the light's power. But he could not, for the light was far stronger than the mystic power he possessed. The light did come from the staff, but its source was not in the staff nor was it the staff itself. Azotus knew this and vanished before their eyes. The Warslingers looked around and the knights appeared with them. The battle was over. Astolat had won.

Some days later, Bernard and Elaine returned to Astolat and started the reconstruction of the city. Bernard had thanked Moses and the Warslingers for their aid and effort. However, Moses did inform Bernard Azotus would not be returning to his city anymore, but he will return one day to exact payment on the lost battle. Bernard understood the Warslinger's words and chose to assist the Heptad against Vorr once the time arises. Elaine hugged Moses and thanked the Warslingers for their help. They had left the city, returning to Old Jerusalem.

On the path back, Arthur turned to Moses, thinking of Vorr and the battle. He knew the answer to his question and Moses knew it as well.

"Was he who I think he was?" Arthur said.

"He was." Moses replied. "A man once one of us. A Warslinger gone to the malevolency."

THE HAUNTED CITY ONE-SHOT
HELPER'S HAND

The small village of Lotnan was quiet, fairly unusual for a place such as it is. Villagers moved throughout the town, going about their daily habits and routines. While do so, a few were startled by the appearance of a sudden figure. Cloaked in his duster and hat. His horse brown as the dirt. The footsteps of the mount gave presence. The villagers knew it was a Warslinger of the Heptad. They each moved from him, giving him nods of respect. The Warslinger nodded back, continuing through the village.

"Please, please help!" Someone screamed in the distance. "I need help!"

A rugged young man ran with speed, approaching the Warslinger. Fear lived in the young man's eyes and the Warslinger could see it clearly. He looked down at the young villager. Discernment kept him focused and his presence keen.

"What appears to be the problem?"

"You're... you're a Warslinger, right?"

"I am."

"There's something lurking around our village. Something terrifying."

"Tell me what it is and I'll deal with it."

"I would, but, you must follow me."

"Follow you?" The Warslinger questioned. "Give me the description of the cause."

"I would, but, it's better if you can follow me back to my home. I'll explain everything there."

The Warslinger stared. He nodded. Humoring the young man as he followed him to his home. His home was near the edge of the village on the other end. The Warslinger jumped from his horse and entered the home. Inside, he saw a young woman and a young girl. Also present were candles, floral material, and other minerals.

"Is this your family?"

"Yes sir."

The Warslinger greeted the woman and the child.

"Where is the problem you spoke of?"

"It's not that easy to describe. Perhaps, I can elaborate in a slow manner."

"Tell me of your concern before I take my leave."

The young man hesitated to say another word as the Warslinger approached him. His presence startled the young man and his eyes were intense. Even the young woman chose to take the child and herself into another room.

"Say it."

"Ok. I brought you out here to stop some bandits."

"Bandits?" The Warslinger said. "Where are your protectors? Isn't it their job to protect?"

"They're being paid off by the bandits. Some say they're in agreement to slaughter the village to ensure complete control over the people."

"A slaughter to gain profit." The Warslinger nodded. "Very well. Where are these bandits located?"

"East of the village."

The Warslinger nodded.

"Then, that is where I must go."

"Sir." The young man said, running toward the Warslinger. "There's nearly a dozen of them. You're just one man. You might need some assistance."

The Warslinger paused and sighed.

"Young one, I've been in enough shooter-fights to determine my survival. dealing with a band of thieves won't be a problem."

The Warslinger exited the young man's home and traveled eastward on the village. Making his stop, he noticed several men. Three of them walking down the main road. The Warslinger stopped his horse and sat by one of the trees, watching the men take their walk. He could hear their conversation. Speaking of such events regarding more raids of livestock, food, and women. He knew they were part of the band of bandits. Therefore, the Warslinger waited until the men led him to their camp. Scouting the area, the Warslinger concluded the camp was full of men. Twelve in total. Keeping his horse a few feet distant from the camp, he loaded his ark shooters and walked into the camp.

"The hell are you supposed to be, strander?" One of the bandits questioned.

The bandits all stood up and walked toward the Warslinger. Their hands on their weapons. From swords to staves and axes. However, one of the bandits stared at the Warslinger. Taking note of his attire from his hat, coat and posture, the bandit began taking steps back. Bumping into his comrades as they shoved him.

"What's your deal?"

"You don't know what he is!"

"Who the hell is he?"

"You seriously don't know? He's one of them."

"One of what?" A bandit asked.

The Warslinger took a step forward, startling the bandits. They cleaned their weapons as the Warslinger stared with a calm focus. The presence of him caused the bandits to question their current circumstance as the warning bandit ran out of the campsite.

"I've heard words of your harassment toward the village of Lotnan."

"Yeah. They have things we need. Things to survive in this desolate world. What gives?"

"Their hard work doesn't deserve the wickedness of your hands."

"Listen, strander. You're interrupting a night of peace. Best you leave us be before you end up in the ground you're standing on."

"So, it's death then?"

"Death it is." The lead bandit said with a touch of cockiness in his voice.

The Warslinger nodded. Raising his hands, holding the arkshooters, he began firing rounds into the bandits. They cowered the campsite in terror as the shots echoed through the air. The Warslinger kept his posture as he pulled the trigger continuously. Reloading after six shots and returning fire. It wasn't long before the entire campsite was silent with only the kindling fire remaining. The Warslinger searched the campsite, seeing eleven of the bandits dead. Their blood pouring into the earth. He nodded and went out into the wilderness in search of the bandit who fled. Traveling not far from the village, the Warslinger eventually found him hiding amongst the villagers. The bandit saw him and dropped to his knees in terror. He held his hands up begging for forgiveness.

"I am not the one who you should be begging for forgiveness."

The villagers ran out of the sight of the Warslinger as he held his arkshooter toward the bandit's forehead. His finger slowly on the trigger as the bandit cried in fear.

"How many of these villagers have you killed?"

"I've… I've killed none."

"None. You're saying it was your associates who did all the evil? The plundering? The raping and the killing?"

"Yes. I suggest we could possibly talk to the villagers, but they refuse. Said using force was a better option."

The Warslinger nodded.

"What is your name?"

"Joseph."

"Well, Joseph, if I let you live this day, do you promise to turn your life around? For the better of not only yourself, but for those who seek peace in their own lives?"

"Yes. Yes I do."

"Very well. I will let you live this day, Joseph. Leave this village and find another place to dwell. When the morning comes, begin your new life. A life I have given you."

"Thank you, Warslinger. I will not forget this."

"I hope not. Because, if I ever receive word of another similar event and you're in the area, I will send you to the Outer-World. Without haste."

Joseph nodded. Quickening in his shoes as the tears flowed.

"Now go."

Joseph had fled the village of Lotnan as the Warslinger returned to the young man's home to fill him in on the news. Hearing the clearing of the bandits brought the young man happiness. For himself, his family, and the village entirely. The villagers received the news and celebrated the Warslinger's helping hand as he rode off, continuing his journey toward The Haunted City.

THE BEASTS OF THE UNKNOWN

<u>THERE WERE GIANTS IN THOSE DAYS</u>

During the age when the earth was filled with violence and wickedness, there not only existed man among the earth, but giants were also present during the time of wickedness. Chanokh was one to witness the giants of renown enter the earth through the means of the Sons of Yah mingling with the Daughters of Man. Through the intermingling, came forth giants and the men of renown.

The giants fought alongside each other through the earth in those days, whereas even Chanokh knew their existence was not to be created nor to be designed. Giants began to form during the time of Queen Alyssa, whom had a giant build her castle and queendom alongside the men who allied with her, believing her false prophecies that were stated to come in the latter days. The giants were later witnessed by many others whom had come into the earth in those days and had seen the trouble that stood before them.

Harold, a man who had witnessed the galactic war between the Dark Gods and the Cosmics, witnessed the giants being used as tools for both legions against one another after Chanokh was taken from the earth to Shemayim by The Most High. The giants had picked sides, stating the winning side would rule the earth for one thousand years in their lifetime. In which, the Dark Gods won and the giants that sided with them became conquerors over the lands in the earth. Until they were overthrown and defeated by Harold, The Cosmics, and The Most High himself.

The Giants later became more corrupt than before. As they would begin to eat the flesh of man and drink their blood. It was during the days of Dore that the end of the Giants would be completed, and their death would be a civil war amongst each other before the flooding water had covered the lands of the earth. During those days, men fought back against the giants with swords, hammers, bows and arrows. The giants had overcome them in their bloody battles before The Most High spoke to Gabriel to cause them to fight each other until they were all dead.

The giants fought one another in a combat of blood and sweat. Giants slaughtering giants across the lands of the earth. For many had become witness to the great towering battles and foreknew it would be the beginning of the end of their time. The giants later rallied other giants to assist them and the civil war had begun. During the civil war, Dore and his family were preparing their vessel in preparation of the deluge that was coming after the civil war. Mankind in general had become partakers and witnesses to the battles of the giants. Some fed into the fights as a form of entertainment.

The mothers and fathers of the giants were weeping at their children killing and slaughtering each other. The fathers, which were the Sons of Yah, petitioned Chanokh to speak with The Most High in an effort of repentance. But, The Most High had rejected the petitioning and they were left to remain and witness their offspring kill each other in fights of bloodlust and rage. The giants fought for years and years. Generations of man that came before and came during were all witnesses to the war of the Giants. From Chanokh to Dore, the giants waged in a civil war.

Many of the Sons of Yah were taken and bind during the final days of the civil war. Unable to see their offspring again as they were taken into the darkness abyss. During those final years, Dore had preached to mankind, speaking of preparation of the water falling from the sky. Mankind mocked Dore as they went about their lives and continued to watch the war of the Giants as entertainment for their own sakes. Alyssa was gone from the earth, Chanokh was gone from the earth, Harold was gone from the earth, and Dore remained on the earth during the last years of the Giants' war.

Some nights, Dore could hear the roaring and smashing of the giants as they fought night and day constantly without any rest due to the spiritual power of the Archangel Gabriel with his order from The Most High. The fallen angels bound into eternal prisons until their appointed judgments. They could still hear their offspring warring and dying in slaughters. Dore spoke with Methus, father of Miykael and grandfather to Dore about the coming deluge and the end of the giants' civil war. Methus foreknew that he would leave the earth and enter the spiritual realm after the giants had killed each other for the deluge to come across the earth. Dore's three sons, Adad, Samael, and Mordecai were also witnesses to the giants' final days of war.

In those last days of the time of the giants in the days of Dore, the giants were at their last. Constantly full of energy and rage in warfare. Dore and his family were set to enter the vessel before the deluge had come. Methus had prepared himself in entering the spirit world and leaving the natural world.

"The time is almost here, grandson." Methus said to Dore. "Once the abominations have killed themselves on the face of the earth, I will leave this world, allowing the deluge to come and wash the earth of its wickedness.

The giants fought to their last breaths as they all killed each other in warfare. The giants were all dead. Methus had passed on into the spiritual world. Dore and his family were set in the vessel as The Most High had closed the door and the deluge came and washed the earth of its wickedness. Forty nights and forty days the waters stood above the grounds of the earth with the wickedness beneath it, grasping for air.

After the waters had settled and Dore's sons had begat their own children with their own wives, a remnant of the giants was left behind. Though, these giants were in heightening size as of the giants that came before. There were giants in the days of Queen Alyssa, Chanokh, Harold, and Dore. But, the giants that came after were great in stature and powerful in strength, but were nothing like the predecessors before them.

The predecessors however, within them were spirits of their own. Their spirits were of evil and had proceeded from their bodies. The evil spirits of the giants afflicted, oppressed, destroyed, attacked, do battle, and work destruction upon the earth and everyone on it, causing trouble. They take no food, but have an everlasting hunger and thirst, which cause offenses.

The spirits of the giants revolted against the children of men and against the women, because they proceeded from them. The spirits of the giants are what are commonly known as demons.

CETUS

The Cetus, a rare beast that has gone throughout history as one of the world's most terrifying creatures to live underneath the deep seas. The Cetus has its rare cases of destroying ships that sail above the oceans and dragging them and their crew deep beneath the sea to drown and later to eat upon. Those who have seen the Cetus with their own eyes depict the beast as a creature of pure malevolence and evil and its presence of great fear and trembling.

The Cetus is usually associated with the Greek God known as Poseidon, who used the Cetus to attack Ethiopia during the Greek era with Cassiopiea boasted of her daughter, Andromeda's beauty above the Nerieds that lived in the deep waters. In the Hebrew Bible, the monster is depicted to be the beast who swallowed Jonah. In the Covenant of Ages, the individual known as Ohm encountered the Cetus and was also swallowed by the beast, only to be freed a few days later. The Cetus is said to have been turned to stone by Perseus during their encounter. There also is a constellation of stars named after the beast itself.

There is one tale that hasn't been spoken about the Cetus that will present itself at this very moment. The time when the battle between the Ostacrean and Magnitran armies in the land of Lelat. During the battle, a warrior who is known as Accladus saw the Cetus with his own eyes before their ships made landfall to face the Ostacrean armies. In Accladus' own words he described the Cetus as a large serpent with eyes that could rip out an individual's soul and throw it deep under the sea until the soul had entered the depths of Hadi, where it would burn for eternity.

"The Cetus' eyes possessed so much darkness that it could suck the soul out of someone's body and throw it deep into the deep sea until it slammed into the ground where it would open, and the soul would be in the dwelling realm of Hadi, who guards the underworld."

There is also the event where the Roman army went into battle with the remaining Greeks and they used the Cetus as a tool for war. Having their soldiers ride on the back of the beast to destroy the Greeks who had ships in the nearby waters. They reviled at the sight of the beast attacking the Greeks and eating their bodies at such quick pace. It even created waves with its body to turn over their ships.

"We can use this creature for our own desires. The creature could possibly help us end this war with those lasting Greeks who continue to thwart our plans of world domination."

The Cetus had later disappeared with many ending tales to its name. People still say they've seen the monster throughout the centuries and decades that have raced over the face of the earth. From the 6th Century to the 19th Century as well into the 20th Century and the 21st Century.

There is also the legend of the Loch Ness Monster, who some believe could very well be the Cetus itself. Though, no evidence has been conclusive enough to determine of the Loch Ness Monster is indeed the Cetus of ancients' old. In the past and present hours, people cling to the idea of a colossal sea monster living beneath the seas that surround the land. People from all parts of the earth come together to tell the stories of their possible encounters with the Cetus while on a ship or near the waters of the sea. There was a quote that an individual said about the Cetus and its future place.

"We will come across the Cetus one day. I know in my heart that we will, and the great legend will be solved once and for all."

The individual continues his search for the Cetus at all parts of the earth where the seas may touch. He seeks the beast and craves its present before his eyes. He also has some companions with him as they all travel together to find the monster and reveal its legendary presence before the modern world. Though, interesting enough, there are tales of the Cetus' return and what its purpose is of returning and its full intent.

"The Cetus will return, and its imposing threat will spread across the globe like a pandemic. People near the seas will regret having their homes placed there as the Cetus will seek to destroy all that they possess. I surely hope they've prepared themselves for the great disaster that awaits them and others who live near the seas' waters."

Some believe the Cetus will be used for good and find a way of saving people trapped at the seas. Others believe that the Cetus is only an animal that has outlived many of its ancient companions and still dwells in the seas of the earth to this day and will do so beyond our time. There are those few who believe that the Cetus will be conjured up from the oceans by an evil force, who will use the beast for its own intended purposes of causing chaos across the globe.

In many books and legends, the Cetus is said to have risen, disappeared, and to return in future days. As sightings of the creature continue to show itself across the globe, many will only wonder if the Cetus will return and cause the chaos that many believe it will or will it return and protect humanity from itself and clean the seas that were once pure of filth and decadence.

"Those of us, who have intelligence and use it wisely, we know that this creature called the Cetus is one of many legends to spread across planet earth. It is our duty and task to find this creature at once before it finds a way to discover us once again and brings about the end of our world."

"Come quickly! The beast has appeared before us in this distressful time we live in. Send the armies to combat the creature as we are in a terrible situation, trapped here in these waters as the beast stares at us. Only the Most High himself can truly help us overcome the threat we currently face. Send your armies at whatever disposal you can. For if you do not, this monster will come to your waters and destroy them as well. For this creature is not of great miracles and spectacles, but of pure hatred and deep malevolence that it possibly cannot be stopped by mortal men. Only Yah can stop the creature, for it is Him who created the world and it is Him who created the Cetus. Praise Yah. Praise YAH!"

THE ENDLESS ONES

The Endless Ones, many do not understand who they are or where they come from. They have been around since time began and are constantly growing in numbers. Created by The Unheard-Of, the Endless Ones scatter across the universe in a variety of ways. Both physically and spiritually. There have been many reports of the Endless Ones in both modern day and history.

Historical accounts describe the Endless Ones as humanoid beings that appear to be transparent in some parts and fully physical in another. One historical accounts, described in Hebrew mentioned the Endless Ones had once taken over the world through The Unheard-Of, when many people began to consume themselves in violence and sodomy. Upon taking over the land, The Endless Ones were worshipped as gods and granted wishes and miracles to their followers. Many of their followers were misguided spirits who were lost and couldn't find their way to the Other Side. Other human beings who opposed the Endless Ones were either tortured or put to death by them or their followers.

Throughout the latter parts of the historical accounts, it stated that their powers began to fade as many humans turned to another source of faith to guide them in the power of the Christ. Upon losing their powers, The Unheard-Of decided to make himself known and showed himself to a large crowd that surrounded the followers of the Endless Ones and gathered them all, including the followers and took them away from the Earth to never return in their physical form.

After that moment in history, there have been slightly no signs of the Endless Ones on the Earth until the later days of the 14th Century when massive accounts of sighting took place. Many believed that the sightings were a sign that they were returning along with The Unheard-Of to destroy the world. But, that was not the case as the sighting were concluded as misguiding and falsely reported to the general population at that time. In latter centuries, sightings continued to be reported, some even by police, military, and political officials at the time. Though, none were taken seriously to consider a proper investigation and search.

In the early 1800s, there were sightings of the Endless Ones described by the witnesses and were fully detailed in drawings of them. Citing their large and strange humanoid shaped features with their rough burgundy red skin that appeared as if it was burned nearly to a crisp and their piercing and deadly glowing yellow eyes. The eyes resemble that of The Unheard-Of, citing that he has endowed them with some abilities of his own to use to their advantage. The drawings made the front page in news across Europe and later found its way across the globe.

Towards the 1900s, near the first World War, people began to assume that the war was started by the Endless Ones causing a stir in dividing countries from another, thus helping one country fight another with their supernatural help and guidance. Many believed the theory to be subtleness and ignored any possible reference or evidence of the Endless Ones aiding a country in the World War. After the war ended, sightings of the Endless Ones began to fade once again as many people moved on with their lives and their current state in faith. It wasn't until near World War II that many people began to realize that supernatural occurrence were taking place, and many believed it was in the form of Adolf Hitler and the Nazi party.

During the 1930s and 1940s, people were in constant fear of Hitler's rise to power by leading Germany into a new World War with a multitude of countries aligning and opposing each other. During one of Hitler's speeches, people said that they witnessed two humanoid beings enter the offices of the location, which is said where the Nazi party were into to discuss their plans in secret.

When Hitler gave his speeches, people reported seeing the Endless Ones standing beside him as he gave out the speeches declaring his plan to rule the world and create a new race of superhuman beings called the Aryans. Many Germans followed suit to Hitler as he led them into World War II. Many people believed that Hitler was given the idea of concentration camps by the Endless Ones to keep the ones who opposed him in line while he continued his plan of world domination.

After World War II, the Endless Ones began to fade again as the Third Reich collapsed, the Aryan race vanishing, and Hitler disappearing from public and military personnel. Afterwards was the creation of the United Nations, as many saw the opportunity of uniting the countries of the world into one singularity form of government. Some speculated that the Endless Ones were seen again near the Vietnam War and even the Cold War. Sightings of the Endless Ones disappeared with many people who believed they even existed and considered their historical accounts to be fairy tale stories passed down through generations.

Later on near the 1980s and 1990s, smaller evidence that indicated the Endless Ones' existence began to give rise to their presence in the world. In the late 1990s, many continue to ignore or even declined information regarding them as they considered it official to be fairy tale stories taken too seriously. Upon the 2000s, as incidents began to occur, few people began to assume that the Endless Ones were making their return to the earth as the faith of many had died out and faded away over time. In today's time, many begin to believe that they are returning and are preparing the return of The Unheard-Of, who will make his presence known in the world and will claim it for himself.

The sunlight beams through the windows of an office. Inside the office are a young boy and an adult man, dressed in white shirt and brown slacks, who's reading out of a book. The young boy sits in a chair with his hand on his chin, looking at the adult man reading from the book.

"You're saying that the Endless Ones are walking around us today and they're about the present The Unheard-Of to the world?" The young boy said.

"Son, I'm only reading from this particular book to give you a better way of understanding things. Though, you won't fully understand it until you get much older."

"So, when I'm older, I'll be able to see the Endless Ones and The Unheard-Of with my own eyes?"

The adult man laughed as he closed the book and placed it onto the nearby bookshelf. He walked over the boy and rubbed him on his head. He kneeled toward him.

"Only time will tell, my son."

CRIES OF THUNDER IN THE SKIES

In the skies, dark clouds form and the thunder roars tremendously above the ground, striking fear and trembling in the hearts of people. The lightning mostly makes its appearance before the thunder introduces itself to the ears of the world. There are many stories that delve into the power and mystery of thunder and lightning. People would seem to disbelieve or disprove anything that could trace toward the power of thunder and lightning.

When people look up into the skies and they noticed the dark clouds forming above them, getting close together and the first small sound of thunder roared, many ran into shelter for protection. The lightning had already made itself known before the thunder roared, yet the people's eyes didn't catch a blink of it. The rain would come falling from the heavens and onto the earth like a colossal shower taking place. When it comes to rain, the differences between people around the world come together. Some love the rainfall, some hate it, and others really have no care for it other than to clean their material wealth that sits outside.

Legends in the earth tell of a large bird that flew, hidden in the dark clouds causing the thunder and lightning to take place amongst the people and the land they live on. This bird is known as the Thunderbird. A colossal bird of great proportions that when it flies, the sound of thunder follows it with its roar and the lightning presents itself like a lighting show. The Thunderbird also has many names across its long and cryptic track record of existence.

The Thunderbird has been seen by many people throughout time and some say they continue to see the creature to this day. Though, none have ever had the opportunity to say if they've ever come face to face with the creature or even attempted to capture it for money or glory. Many Native Americans tell the story of the Thunderbird with detail of its shrouded history. Historians and zoologists have also studied the Thunderbird and could never come up with a solution to its mystery.

"I for one say on this day and time, when the mysterious creature known to us as the Thunderbird makes its presence fully known to the world, that will be the day when all the mysteries of the earth be revealed unto mankind to witness." - Thomas Bradford.

Scientists would usually speculate or throw out the possibility of a Thunderbird existing, let alone flying through the sky creating the sound of thunder and producing lightning from its eyes and wings. They wouldn't believe the possibility of a creature being able to create thunderstorms out of thin air, let alone air that could be filled with dew and possible precipitation. Many of them would say that the individuals or groups that sighted the Thunderbird were only see regular sized birds in large scale due to their binoculars zoomed in or any other theory they could bring up to detest the possibility of the bird's existence.

Some would insist that the Thunderbird was only part of the dinosaur species known as the pterodactyl, due to its appearance and early reports of its sightings in the earth. People have speculated that the Thunderbird could also be an enhanced pterodactyl due to the amount of chemicals in the air or even radiation from the sun or the earth's core.

There is the other theory of there being more than only one Thunderbird living amongst the earth and they travel in various locations, but rarely come together. Many sightings have taken place in Alaska, where people would see the creature flying in the sky above the woodlands. It was usually seen during the winter as it would be searching for prey to consume. There have been other historic legends that regard the Thunderbirds as protectors of the earth that once destroyed reptilian beings that traveled and roamed across the earth.

There are many comparisons between the Thunderbird and the Roc, another colossal bird that is hidden in plain sight. Though, the only sighted Roc would be King Roc that lives not on this earth, but another planet amongst humanoid Roc beings. But, that is for another season to discuss. The Thunderbird and Roc are both large birds with incredible wingspans and able to fly at great speeds.

They can also create hurricane force winds using their wings during flight. Both gigantic birds could snatch an elephant or a whale to eat as food whenever they chose to. The Thunderbird is also spoken about as carrying snakes as its travels in the air.

"There will come a day when the legend of the Thunderbird will no longer be a legend, but a reality among people." - Michael Ledford.

Though, when you look at the world, it is filled and shrouded with mysteries since its inception and creation. If the Most High Yah had created the Thunderbird for its use in creating thunderstorms is mainly unknown to the human mind and far too complicated for the human mind to grasp for understanding. Many who have read the Bible know the Most High uses weather to bring humility unto humans in order for them to understand the sense of fear and trembling, in a way of understanding their place on the earth and existing on this side of glory.

It is understandable that the Most High wouldn't have to create a creature such as the Thunderbird to create thunderstorms to bring humility unto His people. If He did create the Thunderbird, as well as all the other strange and mysterious creatures that have been sighted and continue to roam the earth to this very day, He did it for his own pleasure and no argument can be created to combat the cause and need.

The Most High has created all things that dwell in the earth and out of the earth. Everything was created for his own pleasure and for his own glory. If the Thunderbird is a true creation of the Most High, then it is for his glory that the Thunderbird continues to live and stays shrouded in mystery unto the Age of Revelations unfold and all is revealed unto mankind.

THE BAITAL

In this world, there have been many to have encountered the creature known as the Baital. A large, shaped creature that has the appearance of a human with brown skin and hair with large bat wings on its back and a goat-like tail. Its eyes frighten whosoever lays sight upon it. The Baital attacks its prey vigorously and sometimes kills them without any hesitation or thought. The creature comes from the depths of Hindu Folklore and Mythology and it said to hang itself to trees by its toes, same as the average bats across the world. The name Baital is a variation that comes from the Hindustani word known as "betal". The Baital is said to live in the country of India.

From what is spoken about of The Baital is its skin and facial features. The Baital is said to have a very thin body as if it appeared to be completely stretched across its bones, giving it the impression of an undead body. Old legends have said that its body was near the strength of iron or metal, which would imply that it could not be stopped by any ordinary weapon created by human beings. The Baital possesses either green or red eyes, depending on the area of its location. Its face appears like a dried-up coconut as some would say. By staring into its eyes, people could tell that there was no life-force within the vessel nor did its eyes ever give off a twinkle of any kind. Within the Indian culture, brown is associated with fiends and witches.

The Baital has no blood of its own within its body. Instead

its takes over the dead bodies of many who have died and were buried underneath the tree that The Baital possessed and marked as its own territory. Some would believe that The Baital is a vampire of ancient origin, though The Baital does not drink the blood of its victims.

The Baital is also said to tell stories of its history with a king known as King Vikram, who constantly batted with The Baital in ancient times. Vikram had made a promise to a sorcerer that he would capture The Baital. Of course, Vikram had faced many odds and challenges along the way in his process of trying to capture The Baital for the sorcerer. The Baital proved itself as a match for Vikram as tales of riddles would ensue and keep Vikram in a constant trap as The Baital was content in its present state. The countless battle between the two would last through the cycle of capture and release.

"I cannot bear this no longer." Vikram had said concerning the riddles of The Baital. "I must overcome this task of confronting the Baital. I have to."

Vikram's conquest of The Baital lasted for a total of twenty-five times as he returned to The Baital's marked tree and dealt with the riddles and questions thrown upon him to answer. After the situations that erupted during the events of Vikram and The Baital, The Baital itself vanished into the spirit realm. Some accounts have said of The Baital's whereabouts are known to those who seek it.

"If we try hard enough and focus with great concentration and strength, we can find this Baital and the realm where it hides from open eyes. We can use its power to do whatever we so desire."

How can one find The Baital without knowing the proper place and location to seek and search for it? How would one truly know The Baital's intentions in this present world as it is unlike the world of King Vikram. There are many servants of the Most

High who see The Baital as an enemy and a servant to the Unheard-Of. The Baital is not of any godly consent nor will it ever be of any godly consent. Judging by its appearance, its stature, and its character, The Baital is a celestial creature that is bent on causing devastations to anyone who attempts to seek its presence.

"We must find a way to capture this creature. How can we know for certain what is taking place amongst the spiritual realm when we have no eyes inside?"

The early tales of The Baital were written in ancient Sanskrit, which is a primary language among Hinduism. The twenty-five events between Vikram and The Baital were written and captured in a book of twenty-five tales and legends, concerning the two battling it out with riddles and questions to be answered amongst each other. The time and date that The Baital had its encounters with King Vikram were recorded in the 1st Century BC and some recordings of the encounters continue into the 11th Century, where all of the recordings were compiled and put together as a complete set.

In today's times, many would wonder where The Baital could be hiding in this present world. The Baital could still be inside its country of origin, India. The Baital could be wandering across the globe, traveling to each country, seeking out a victim of its own to choose and cause madness. Though, it is not said if The Baital would return in the End Days and we do not exclude its theory, for The Baital could be used as one of the Unheard-Of's servants and warriors in the Final Battle at the Land of the Forbidden where the forces of The Unheard-Of collide with the forces of the Most High Yah in a battle that will transformation all of creation as we know it.

The Baital marks its tree of territory and continues to use the corpses that lie underneath its tree for its own purposes. Remember, The Baital is not a vampire by any means or stretch of the imagination, no matter how its outer physical presence may have seemed to appear in front of your eyes. To this very day, people would still say they've seen The Baital and some may have ultimate proof of their encounter with the creature. They may see an animated corpse that may have risen from The Baital's tree. Whoever shall see The Baital in person and in its full form, they must prepare themselves for an overflow of questions and riddles to be answered and solved.

THE COMING WRAITHS

The planet called earth is surrounded and covered with spiritual beings that travels throughout the universe and the spiritual plane of existence. These spiritual beings can shift into human beings, extraterrestrials, animals, or any other source that they can model their shift after. These spiritual beings could be angels, demons, or wraiths. The Wraths are the majority of those that shift into other beings to cause and lead others either astray or lead them to something of great ancient importance. The word Wraith arrives from the ancient Norse word, "*Vordr*", which means "*Guardian*" in the English tongue and translation.

Wraiths would usually appear to those who are near death or even after their death will appear before those who are surrounding the deceased earthly body, leaving them as just empty husks of flesh and blood. Wraiths are ghost-like entities that some would call phantoms, specters, apparitions, manifestations of the dead. Other names for them are Soul-Stealer, since they appear before one's death to enter the eternal realm of either peace or torment. The primary trait of the Wraiths is to travel amongst the earth with a driven purpose to consume and capture the souls and spirits of humans. Look at today's people and the Wraiths are doing an excellent job in their line of duty.

Many of the Wraiths would possibly confuse the living into doing their own will instead of doing the will of the Eternal One. The Wraiths can transform a human spirit and soul into a wraith of its own, therefore it will become simply one of them. A member of the Wraith Clan and under the control of the Unheard-Of.

Most Wraiths are under the control of the Unheard-Of. Just as the Endless Ones are under his control, as well as the Kingdoms of the Earth, so are many of the Wraiths.

"What you gaze before you are my Wraiths. They do my biddings to please me for bring humanity to its knees to worship me. For I will be like the Most High and I will ascend to His throne and claim it for myself. I am the Unheard-Of."

The true physical or astral appearance of the Wraiths are mainly all black or mostly a large black fog or cloud that either has a pair of eyes or doesn't have any eyes. Some have mouths and other do not have mouths. The ones with eyes can see and the ones without eyes aren't able to see, but are guided by the Unheard-Of through his own vision. The ones with mouths can speak words of a sweet and pleasurable nature, only used to deceive the illiterate ones. The ones without mouths can use telepathy to communicate with a human being through their mind and are able to read their thoughts and in near control over their conscious.

They hide in dark, deep caves and forests throughout the twelve hours of the day and rise out of the darkness to torment and to deceive during the twelve hours of the night. The demons take over the day and leave the night to the Wraiths as the demons take time to torment those in their sleep and those who aren't on the right side with the Eternal One. The Wraiths can release a loud screech similar to the screech of a banshee. The screech will create and build up fear in the hearts and minds of humans, both male and female.

"The screech became so intensity and unable to bear that I ran out of my home and into the nearest ditch to cover myself from its torturous yell."

The true way of knowing their presence is by the sight of dark clouds. The temperature will drop exponentially, and the Wraith will be known before whosoever is in its presence. Sure, the person might be near freezing due to the fast drop in temperature, but they will surely heat up when their gaze hits the Wraith in its eyes. For surely what would someone do if they encountered a Wraith. One question they should ask is why have they met a Wraith. Have they asked for something greater to seek after in this finite life or have they disobeyed the Eternal One to achieve something for their self-will and self-indulgence?

I, Michael Ledford have yet to encounter a Wraith. I've encountered stupid people amongst all things and yet, I can see the demonic and wicked spirits that live among them and inside them. Once, I was like them, I lived after the manners and pleasures of this wicked world. I desired only what I wanted and what I sought after for my own self. I was all about myself, until I was hit with a spiritual awakening and found myself doing the will of the Eternal One and forsaking all that I had before me.

Now, I am truly a new creature and I no longer do what my own will suggests and throws into my mind. The spiritual awakening brought me closer to the Eternal One and I dearly and truly hope when I see the King coming down from the clouds along with the New Jerusalem out of Shamayim, will the Wraiths finally be put to rest for all eternity with their associates both on earth and in the spiritual realm, and along with their leader, the Unheard-Of when the King and His people rule the earth for one thousand years in peace.

Surely, you're thinking to yourself, this can't all be possible or you're thinking there's no Wraiths or Eternal One and yet, people like you do not bother to do the proper research and study to confirm it for yourself. Neither do you ask the Eternal One for wisdom and understanding. I'm speaking plainly to those who ask questions, but refuse the answers given to the damn questions they asked. The reprobate minded ones. There, that's what they are.

But, to those who truly seek after the will of the Eternal One and continue to do battle within the confounds of spiritual warfare, continue your worship and prayers. For the Wraiths, the Endless Ones, the stupid humans, the demons, and the Unheard-Of will try anything to get your minds off serving and worshiping the true King of the Universe with all diligently.

FORESEEN THE BUNYIP

The Bunyip is a strange creature within the realm of cryptozoology and mythology that is said to lurk within swamps, billabongs, creeks, riverbeds, and waterholes. Some claim the creature to be a water spirit, a spirit that dwells within the Murray River of Australia, its longest river within the Australian Alps. The Moorundi people that live near the Murray River have claimed to see the creature and that it can change its shape and form before the year 1847. Some have claimed the Bunyip to be a giant starfish that lived in the Murray River. Others have stated to be in a sense of dread that they can no longer describe its appearance to those who ask of it.

Many newspapers in the 19th Century describe the creature with a crocodile-like head, a dog's face, dark fur, walrus-like horns or tusks, depending on the witness, a duck's bill, flippers, and a horse-like tail. Reports in 1851 indicate that the Bunyip was killed by a spear after it killed an Aboriginal man. Early settlers of Australia claimed to have seen the creature during their arrivals to the continent. Many believed the Bunyip to be a creature that awaited discovery.

Hamilton Hume in 1818 stated to have found large bones, but did not call it the bones of the Bunyip as some had suggested it to be. Hume and his partner, James Meehan described the bones relating to a hippopotamus or manatee. There were fossils found in the Wellington Caves in 1830 by George Rankin, a bushman. Others were later found by Thomas Mitchell. The word *Bunyip* came along in July of 1845. An Australian museum stated to possess the skull of a Bunyip in 1847. William Buckley wrote an account of the creature in his biography in the year of 1852.

In other times after 1852, the Bunyip was said to have been spotted by those who crossed the Australian Alps such as Gabriel Kane, the Monster Hunter and Ufologist during his early studies of becoming a member of the Symbolum Venatores. Kane spoke to his masters of the creature thereafter, only leaving it remaining alive near the Murray River where he witnessed it. Other hunters came across the creature during their studies. Some went to fight it, but lost in the end to the power of the creature.

Many monster hunters made it their mission between 1852 to 1886 to find the Bunyip, yet failed to do so. Others claimed to have seen the creature but were unable to fight it themselves.

"How can we fight a creature that can change its shape and size? Its form? One minute, it shows itself as a hybrid of many animals that come across the waters of Murray River. Later it appears as if it's an enormous starfish that washed along into the River from the Sea. The next minute it turns itself into some spirit, a water demon perhaps, but not so sure on that matter. In time, Hunters, such as ourselves will confront this creature and then we will have foreseen the Bunyip for what it truly is. Rather it be a natural creature or a spiritual one."

ROAR OF THE WERETIGER

There is a beast that scatters throughout the jungles of Asia with the power and strength of a tiger and the intellect of a human being, which would be great cleverness. This hybrid creature is known to Us as the Weretiger. The Weretiger is spoken about in many ancient folklores and mythologies. They share a great similarity with werewolves and possibly werefoxes and werebears.

The Weretiger goes throughout the day looking like an average human being walking amongst other humans. It is not till nightfall, where it transforms into the Weretiger and begins a bloody massacre by killing anything that comes across its eyesight. The Weretiger has a great thirst for blood in any form possible within the jungles of Asia. Many have come across the beast and only a few have survived the encounter to tell their side of the story when it came across the Weretiger.

There are certain rituals that Asians have taken up to try to transform themselves into Weretigers and scatter the jungles of Asia. Only a few had received the terrible end of the ritual by becoming sick and thrown out into the jungles for the Weretiger to kill and consume. The Weretiger's body is set up as a brute creature with an incredible amount of strength and intelligence. The body of the Weretiger include its long sharp teeth, its slashing long claws, incredible feat of senses with its eyes, nose, ears, and mouth. With its teeth and claws, it can cause deadly bites and devastating slashes. Unlike average tigers, the Weretiger possesses in tail on its body.

The only possible way to transform into a Weretiger is to be bitten by one. Depending on the person who transformers, they either seek revenge on someone or they have an intense craving for power and violence. Maybe the craving for ruling is in there as well.

The Weretiger is said to have started in the areas of India before being spread over into the jungles of Asia, where it currently remains dormant from modern day civilizations. There was a group of explorers and people of adventure who traveled into the deep jungles of Asia to search out the Weretiger and reveal its presence to the world. They were named Gates, Laura, Kenny, Kathy, Rex, and Jude. Gates was the leader of the group as they entered the jungles.

The jungles are covered with massive trees and slithering insects looking for food and places to rest. Gates finds a location near a large rock where he and his group set their camp for the night. The group place their bags and equipment together at the rock where Rex will stay and watch the cameras during the night with Kathy.

"Ok, Laura will be with me and Kenny, you're with Jude."

"Alright then." Kenny said. "Let's get this mission done."

Gates, Laura, Kenny, and Jude walk into the jungles and split up. Two to Two. Gates and Laura went east, Kenny and Jude went west. All they could see in front of them was pure darkness apart from the moonlight shining through the trees. Gates reached into his cargo pants pocket and pulled out some night-vision glasses. He had two in his hand and gave one to Laura.

"Put this on. It should help you watch your steps." Gates said. "The moonlight shines and, yet we can only see darkness in front of us and there's no telling where the Weretiger is at this moment."

"Who knows, Gates, we could come across the beast

ourselves and hopefully not be killed."

"We'll see about that once we face the beast."

Kenny and Jude continued walking west on their side of the jungles. Jude noticed some very large footprints on the ground in the muddy dirt. She lowered herself to have a better look at the footprint. Kenny stopped as he saw her studying the print.

"What did you find?" Kenny asked.

"This footprint is larger than any known animal in this jungle. Look at the size of its paw to its nails. This isn't an ordinary tiger we're dealing with here."

"Of course not, lady. We're out here to search and find the legendary beast known as the Weretiger. Which it would be incredible to capture it and reveal it to the world."

"That's if we can capture it. It has the cunningness and intelligence as a human being."

"Sometimes, even human beings are able to be easily fooled and captured by their hunters."

Rex and Kathy sat at the campsite, where they watched on the cameras most of the jungles. Nothing was showing itself on the camera and it was dead silent. Rex continued to glance at all four cameras and still nothing was seen.

"Anytime now we should come across something." Rex said. "This jungle is too big not to have some form of movement."

"We still have a few hours of searching and we should encounter this animal. Be it a tiger, a panther, or the Weretiger itself." Kathy said.

Gates and Laura kept walking through the darkness with their night-vision glasses on and their small digital cameras in hand through the jungles until they reach what appeared to be a small creek. Gates stopped walking as so did Laura. He scouted the area for any sign of life moving.

"Didn't know there was a creek out here." Gates said.

"No telling what you'll find out here, Gates."

They searched around their side of the creek, hearing only the slight sounds of owls hooting in the trees and fish swimming in the creek. Gates looked down and saw the same kind of footprint that Jude saw with Kenny. Laura looked down at the footprint as Gates searched for samples of hair, saliva, or blood.

"Think that's its footprint?" Laura said.

"It could be. Look at the size of it. Unless we're dealing with an enlarged tiger or panther, this could possibly be the footprint of the Weretiger. Which means it's within this jungle tonight."

After Gates took the samples and placed them inside a plastic bag that he put into his shirt pocket, a loud shriek of a roar is heard throughout the jungle. The entire group hears the roars and knows it's not from an ordinary animal. Gates looked around himself and Laura forming a 360 degree circle.

"We have to find the location where that roar came from!" Gates said. "Let's go!"

Gates and Laura ran through the jungle, following the sound of the roar as it can still be heard. Kenny and Jude decide to also track down where the roar was coming from as Rex and Kathy at the campsite were completely glued to the cameras for any sign of movement.

"That roar should've woken up most of this jungle's inhabitants." Rex said. "We are about to see a lot of movement taking place."

On the cameras, Rex and Kathy spot several shapes

moving past the cameras. They paused one of their cameras and looked to see that it was a pack of orangutans that ran across the camera, going through the trees, away from the roar's location. The other three cameras showed constant movement from animals such as the Silvery Gibbon, the Proboscis Monkey, a Slender Loris, and on the ground, a couple of snakes slithered past the cameras. But, no sign of the Weretiger was found on the camera.

"No Weretiger, Kathy." Rex said. "Dammit."

After a brief second of silence, they heard a thumping sound that came from nearby their campsite. Rex and Kathy each sat still as the thumping sound inched closer toward them. They sat quietly as the thumping sound turned into a large object that they could see with their own eyes. The object stood still as it stared at Rex and Kathy and gave off a small roar. Rex listened closely and noticed it wasn't the Weretiger and he squinted his eyes and saw it was only a Sumatran Rhinoceros. The Rhinoceros turned its head and continued to walk past the campsite. Rex and Kathy are relieved by the Rhinoceros' appearance.

Back in the jungle, Gates and Laura find themselves deeper in the jungle where the roar is right next to them. They hear rusting in the trees and they turn to see both Kenny and Jude. They all catch their breath.

"Looks like we ran into your zone." Kenny said.

"Just trying to find what is giving off that roar." Gates said. "We have to keep moving."

Gates' communicator sounded off as he answers it. Rex is on the other side of the talkie. Gates answers Rex's call.

"What is it, Rex?"

"We saw large amounts of animals scattering through the jungle and you have to watch yourselves."

"You're telling us this now instead of earlier?"

"We have a little incident of our own over here with a Sumatran Rhinoceros. We saw a rhinoceros."

"Good call, but did you see anything that could lead toward the Weretiger because that's why we're all out here?"

"No, we didn't capture footage of the Weretiger. Sorry, Gates."

Gates sighed as he turned to Laura, Kenny, and Jude. He told Rex to stay on standby just in case something else would come along. He tells them that they only have about thirty minutes left before sunrise and they must find the Weretiger before then. Now, all four of them stay together in a group as they quickly search around the jungle for the Weretiger.

Now, with only twenty minutes remaining, the group is becoming more intolerant of the Weretiger's whereabouts. Gates is constantly fighting off the idea of calling off the mission and returning to camp.

"We have to keep searching with whatever means we can have." Gates said to himself.

Rex communicated back with Gates again through the talkie as Gates responded to his call.

"Anything this time, Rex?"

"Yeah. We just saw something very large walk past the camera and its heading toward your direction."

"What did it look like, Rex?!"

"It looked like a fairly large brute and it didn't look like a friendly type of animal, Gates."

"Thanks, Rex."

"Watch yourselves out there, Gates and company."

They hear the roar again and it appeared to be closer than they originally imagined. Kenny pointed toward the trees in front of them as they began to rustle and shake. The branches of the trees began to break and fall to the ground where the dirt would fly up into the air at mid-range.

They saw a large beast walk out of the trees, with a stick in hand that appeared to be made from the skulls and spines of both a human being and a ram. The beast stood on its hind legs to the estimated height of twelve feet. Its teeth were sharper than any other animal that lived in the jungle and its eyes pierced the group like death on swift wings. The group could only stare in intensely and stay in complete silence as they stared at the beast and its large brute figure. The beast stated at the group and raised its head toward them and gave off a roar. The group had fully recognized that roar and Gates could only believe as the sun began to rise, removing his night-vision glasses.

"Guys, this is the Weretiger. This is the roar of the Weretiger."

TRAVIS VAIL, SPIRIT-SEEKER: FIRST SINS

I

WHAT CAME BEFORE

Reading through his past investigations and encounters with the otherworldly, Travis Vail, known in the occult circles as the Spirit-Seeker, is researching more of his past encounter with Kamagrauto, the demon who opened his mind to the larger world. After the visitation from Kamagrauto at the Black Raven Hotel and in finding the Mutant-Thing, Vail is curious about the world he's about to enter. A world where the supernatural comes into conflict with the rising heroes. A mixture that will only end in chaos.

Still studying, Vail's phone rang, and he answered with slight haste and ease of movement. His instincts were still kicking. His mind on Kamagrauto's words and his encounter with Abraham and The Swordman.

"Vail speaking."

"Trav, good to hear your voice."

"Ah. Dr. Galen Donovan." Vail said with a smirk. "Same here. Why have you called?"

"I have a case for you. If you're interested."

"What kind of case if I may ask humbly?"

"From what I've learned, it concerns the first sins?"

"First sins? As in the first sins committed after the Fall?"

"Correct."

Vail nodded. "I'm on board. Send me the details and I'll follow suit."

"Will do." Donovan said. "You'll have the information shortly."

Vail hung up and within several minutes, the information was sent to Vail through his email. Reading the files, Vail learned the first sins were moving through the world in slow form. Unusual to his previous encounters in past cases, there was a map attached to the files which detailed the past locations of the sins' movements. Vail packed his gear, what was needed, grabbed his black trench coat and left his lair.

Following the map's layout, Vail went across most of the United Kingdom into France and into Germany. Vail has spoken with several witnesses to the sightings and they explained the sins appeared as one. Embodied to moving around single filed. Whatever it was, it had no motives other than to terrorize and to instill fear into the humans it came across. After each movement it made, the more aggressive it became. From startling humans to torturing them if came close.

"This is something else." Vail noted. "Something far more powerful is at work here than just some series of haunting."

Vail continued his investigations and interviews for the next several days. During those days, Vail began to come across what looked to be plague doctors. Crouched in the shadows to walking past him in crowds. Vail took nothing from it until he managed to see one staring at him from the distance. The plague doctor dressed in an all-black robe. Covered from head to toe with its doctor's mask sticking out of its hood. Vail smirked.

"You think that frightens me, lad? Tell you what, take off that beak and we'll settle this like men."

The plague doctor stood still. Vail waited, yet, nothing came from the doctor.

"Figures." Vail said. "I'm going on about my business. Don't try to follow or you'll end up somewhere you won't like."

Vail contacted Donovan concerning the case and the uprising of plague doctors. Donovan stated the doctors are probably the result of the sins' travels. The doctors are following the path of the sins.

"They may be, but, there's something more to all of this. Something sinister at work."

"Why don't we meet up and discuss our ideas on this case?"

"Sure. Where are you right now?"

"In Italy."

"Let me guess, Venice."

"I'm having a word with Ms. Belinda Grazio. You remember her I presume?"

"I can't forget a face like hers. Anyhow, I'm leaving Germany. I'll be there as fast as possible."

"Take your time. Belinda is patient of your coming."

"She would be."

II

<u>WHAT CAME AFTER</u>

Vail entered the city of Venice near nightfall. Vail had walked through Venice reaching the hotel. When Vail came closer, he could see Donovan standing outside of a door.

"There he is." Vail said walking.

Vail made his way toward Donovan and the two hugged.

"You came quicker than I expected."

"I was on the move right after our conversation."

"Good timing."

"Not my best, but I try."

Vail investigated the hotel room. He saw no one inside. He gazed his eyes toward Donovan while pointing into the room. Donovan looked back into the room and turned to Vail.

"Looking for something?"

"I thought you said Belinda was here?"

"She's at her home." Donovan said. "She will meet with us in the morning. In the meantime, you and I need to discuss this case."

"Sure thing."

Vail entered the hotel room and Donovan followed. Inside, they sat at the coffee table. Atop the table were files Donovan had brought with him. The same documents he emailed to Vail to begin with. Donovan had passed Vail a bottle of beer and Vail drank.

"Plague doctors?" Donovan asked with confusion.

"I saw them at every location the sins had come across. They just stood there. Staring. I taunted one."

"Sounds like something you'll do."

"What would you do if you had a plague doctor staring down at you from across the area?"

"Where did the doctor go?"

"Not sure. I walked away afterwards. Warned it if it followed me it would end up in a far worse place."

"What is your conclusion so far?"

"These areas are connected. The sins aren't traveling by themselves. It's as if they're merged into one. Like they've become an entity."

"You believe the sins have become a living entity? Your presumption I'm assuming?"

"It would explain this more clearly. Besides, the only way for the sins to have merged into an entity, it would need to be brought together by someone of a darker power."

"What of that demon you encountered at Black Raven Hotel? Could he be responsible for this?"

"Wouldn't surprise me. However, he was keen on something else. Regarding myself and others like me in the field."

"How would it know of your future to start with? Demons

aren't that intelligent when it comes to one's future. The past they're aware of."

"That demon was more powerful than our usual demons. This one claimed to be a lieutenant demon who worked for somebody called Dagor The Soul Eater."

"The Soul Eater?" Donovan jumped. "He hasn't been seen since the Middle Ages."

"Well, if his lieutenant is bumping around the world, he mustn't be hidden anymore."

"Your words are true." Donovan nodded. "Well, once we meet Belinda tomorrow, she'll tag along with us on this case."

"No offense, but, why is she interested in this case? I'm sure she has plenty of cases in this city."

"She wanted this case to work with you again. Though, not as I expect it to be. We're not going to Poveglia this time."

"Noted." Vail stood up from the table. "I'm going to get myself a room in this place. I'll speak to you in the morning."

"Sure thing, Travis. Good night."

"Same to you." Vail left Donovan's hotel room.

While Vail had obtained his own room, he walked down the hallway toward the room. Before he could put the key in, Vail spotted another plague doctor standing at the end of the hall. Cloaked in darkness. Yet, its' beak was glowing. Vail sighed.

"You choose to do this now?" Vail asked. "I would like some kind of answer here."

The doctor kept still. Vail shook his head and rubbed his hands together.

'Guess I'll have to make you."

Vail moved with haste toward the doctor and once he reached him, the doctor had vanished into a thin dark mist. Vail searched the surroundings and found nothing.

"This nonsense is something else."

Vail returned to his room and unlocked the door. He entered and went to sleep.

III

<u>WHAT CAME BETWEEN</u>

The following morning, Travis Vail and Galen Donovan entered a café and inside sitting was Belinda Grazio. They noticed, and Vail only sighed as they approached the table and sat down.

"I know." Belinda said. "You're thrilled to see me again."

"I know why you're here." Vail said. "Besides, that's not why I'm here."

"She's here to assist us on this case."

"I'm aware. So, let's get to it shall we."

"Fair enough." Donovan said. "We need your skills to help us solve this case around the first sins."

"The first sins? That's your case?"

"Can you help is the question." Vail pointed out. "Can you?"

"I can help. Only if I can come along with the two of you."

"She would do this." Vail said.

"You can."

"*Prego*." Belinda said. "Glad we can work together again."

"I'm sure you are." Vail said. "Now, can we discuss this case?"

"Yeah. What do you mean by the 'first sins'?" Belinda asked.

"Travis can give you the details. It is his case after all."

"Sure thing. I've come across a number of plague doctors recently and all pf them have some sort of connection to the first sins."

"Like all of them?"

"Yes."

"And you want to find out where these doctors are going and who could be leading them?"

"Precisely. Which is why Galen decided to speak to you. Believing you could be of service to solving this obscure case."

"Well, I can be of service."

"Excellent. Help us and you can go on your way." Vail said.

"What is the plan for today?"

"Since I was visited by a plague doctor last night, I figured we make a trip back to the hotel and search the area. Perhaps, the quiet doctor left something for us to find."

"Well then, I will gather my things and meet you there."

Vail nodded as Belinda hugged Donovan and left the café. Vail turned to Galen, shaking his head.

"Is it always going to be like this with the two of you?" Donovan asked.

"As long as she focuses on the mission, everything will run smoothly."

"And if not?"

"Then, we will have problems. Delays. Something this job doesn't require us to have."

Vail and Donovan left the café and as they walked down the sidewalk, they stumbled across a pair of street preachers. Dressed in bright colors with the menorah and the Star of David on their clothing. They carried with them signs and a chart, detailing locations of the earth. Vail approached them, glancing at the chart.

"And what is this?"

"What do you think, Esau." The preacher said.

"Heh, Esau now." Vail uttered. "Is that what you just called me?"

"Esau is the white man. You are the Devil!" The Preacher yelled.

"Me the Devil? Look here, fellow, the only one of us who's truly the Devil is you and your gang of deceivers."

"Deceivers?! Read the Word, Esau!"

The Preacher looked, seeing Donovan approaching them next to Vail. The Preacher's eyes glanced back and forth between Vail and Galen.

"My brother, you can't be hanging around with the enemy."

"The enemy? This man is my friend."

"You can't be friends with Esau, my brother. Look at this chart right here."

Donovan looked at the chart and nodded. Facing the preacher and his brothers-in-arms.

"I have a solution to the problem. Mind if I speak it to you?"

"Yes sir."

"If the white man is truly Esau, then he is your brother."

"What do you mean by that?"

"Esau was born from Isaac's loins. Thereby, Esau is in fact a

Hebrew."

"That's not what we're discussing, my brother. The white man is the Devil and the white man is Esau."

"Then, if Esau is the white man and the white man is the Devil, you should get busy at casting the Devil out of him. Free him from the demonic troubles."

The preacher stepped back, grabbing a hold of the Bible in hand. He shook his head.

"We can't help those who's minds have been wiped by the white man. We can't. You're a lost cause, my brother. I am deeply sorry. But, I hope **Yahawashi** has mercy on you and grants you entrance when he returns."

"As do I." Donovan said.

"Heh." Vail chuckled. "Hmm."

The two walked away as the preacher continued his preaching. They turned, entering an alleyway. Vail laughed, and Donovan shook his head.

"Didn't think they would be here." Vail said.

"They're growing. Besides, it's part of the endgame."

"As are many things happening today."

From there, smoke arose from the ground, startling the two. A thick black smoke.

"What is this?" Donovan asked.

"I know who it is."

From the smoke came Kamagrauto, the lieutenant demon. Cloaked in its robe and hood. Its eyes visible from the shadow and its horns spiked out. Kamagrauto levitated over the smoke. His legs could not be seen.

"Travis Vail. Galen Donovan. How intriguing it is to find you both here."

"Is that the demon you talked about?" Donovan asked.

"Yeah. That's him."

Kamagrauto glanced at Vail and Donovan. Its hands held together with his long, sharp, and dirty claws.

"Alright, what do you want?" Vail asked.

"To warn you of your current mission. You will not succeed."

"Is that so?"

"Your future depends on this case and I already know, you will fail. The first sins alone are far too vast for Travis Vail to solve on his own. You need guidance. Guidance from the other side and I can provide such."

"I understand your nobility. But, me and Galen have this under control."

"Oh, you do?" Kamagrauto gestured. "Then, I will be watching your every move and when you desire my aid and you will, I will make myself known unto you and those who will be at your side when the moment comes."

"What moment?" Vail asked.

"You will know. You will know."

Kamagrauto vanished into the smoke by falling. The darkness cleared from the alleyway and there was nothing remaining.

"That demon is noble?" Donovan asked.

"He has honor. I know. Strange for a demon to possess such a moral trait."

"Well, there are things not even we can comprehend."

"True. But, someday, I hope we can. Right now, we need to go and meet Belinda."

Making their return to the hotel, Belinda waited for them. She saw the looks on their faces.

"What happened?"

"We came across a demon." Donovan said.

"Or the demon came to us." Vail added.

"What kind of demon?"

"The lieutenant kind."

"That's not making any sense, Travis."

"I'm afraid it is true, Belinda. It's the same demon Travis met at the Black raven Hotel some time ago."

"Kamagrauto? Here?"

"Oh, you know his name." Vail chuckled.

"I thought you were only seeing things. I didn't expect him to exist."

"Well, lass, he exists and trust me, he's not one you would like to meet. Ask Galen of the encounter."

Donovan looked to Belinda and shook his head.

"Kamagrauto is not the typical demons we face. He is something far more ancient and we could feel his power."

"But, do not fret. He offered to help us."

"I hope you refused."

"Not the slightest. He told me whenever I needed his help involving this case, which he is aware of. So, I assume there are others in the spirit world who are familiar with this and aren't giving us any help. Kamagrauto told me to call on him if I needed his aid."

"But, you won't. we'll solve the first sins together."

"True. But, then again, stranger things have happened in this line of work."

Vail walked to the hotel room door.

"I'm going to return to my room and get ready for the work we have to do. I won't be long."

Vail left the room. Belinda turned to Donovan with uncertainty expressing from her face. Galen knew it and sat down.

"What's with him?"

"What do you mean? That's the way he works. Travis is a very different kind of occult detective."

"Yeah. Not one I would assume to have help from a demon. An ancient one at that."

"Why don't you go and talk to him. See what he tells you."

"He already doesn't want me here."

"And that is more reason for you to talk to him. Get through to him. I know it's possible."

"How so?"

"Because I am the one who trained him in this field. His mentor in a way. Anyway, go and speak with him. It'll give us enough time to prepare to find these plague doctors."

Belinda approached Vail's hotel room door and immediately the door opened. Vail stared at Belinda and she did the same. No words.

"What do you want?" Vail asked.

"Can we talk? For just a second."

Vail sighed as he allowed Belinda into his room. Shutting the door behind, Belinda stood, and Vail walked over to the table and sat down. He gestured his hand toward the other seat. Belinda sat with him.

"What?"

"What's with you?"

"How do you mean?"

"I mean your demeanor, your attitude. What's the problem?"

"There's plague doctors roaming around with the first sins on their back. I have to find out who's causing this and way."

"That's not what I'm talking about."

"Then I'm confused."

Belinda sighed.

"Why couldn't it have worked between us, Travis? Why didn't you bother to give it a chance?"

"You are not seriously asking me about relationship details right now."

"I am."

"Women always want to talk."

"Only if the men would listen to our words."

"I'm not trying to build up bitterness in my heart, lass. Besides that, I've told you before. A relationship with me won't work."

"Why not?"

"Because when I was young, I was visited by an angel. The angel warned me not to get married. Otherwise, tragedy would follow. Now, I see what the angel meant. Me traveling on this road of life. Dealing with the supernatural daily. Heh, if I did have a wife, she would've most likely divorced me or been killed in the process."

"But, there's always a way."

"Even though you're in this line of work, tragedy still strikes. The fact of Kamagrauto confronting me, proves the angel's point."

"Well, did this angel have a name?"

"He did."

"What was it?"

"Hmm. Michael."

"As in Michael the Archangel."

"Correct. Funny enough, he's been overseeing my activities since I was a little boy. No worries. However, I am keen on the fact he hasn't intervened with my confrontations with Kamagrauto. Maybe time will tell this course."

Vail sighed. Standing up from the chair, he grabbed his coat from the back of the chair, putting it on.

"Now, let's continue this case of ours."

IV

<u>WHAT CAME WITHIN</u>

Vail and Belinda met with Galen, who found the two of them together somewhat odd, but never the case. They moved forward with the case and after studying the trail of the plague doctor that Vail saw, a clue was given. A name connected to a series of plague doctor sightings. Belinda had the name.

"What is it?" Vail asked.

"Here's the name of the recent plague doctor sightings. All from witnesses who've seen the doctors and later a man would come and visit them. Asking about the doctors before they ever went public with a concern."

"The man's name." Donovan said. "What was it?"

"Timothy Ellis."

"Timothy Ellis. I've never heard of him before."

"I have." Vail said. "It's familiar to my ears."

"What do you know of this man, Travis?"

"He's deeply into the spiritual arts. Mystic stuff as well. But, in the occult circles, he doesn't go by that name. he is known and referred to as Balthazar."

"Is this the mage Balthazar a few have talked about?"

"It is. Balthazar is a mage. A powerful one. Took the name from the biblical magi. Cloaked in his dark-orange hood and robe, he gained power from a deep malevolent force. One of which I am unknown to. But, in time I will find out."

"So, where is Balthazar?" Belinda asked.

"New York City." Vail said. "Which means we have some traveling to do and in little time."

"Yeah, but how long before he finds out we're on to him?"

Vail turned and noticed a shadow hovering in the distance. He stared, and it revealed its eyes.

"Not long." Vail said, staring at the shadow.

"What is it?" Belinda said, turning to also see the shadow.

"What is that?" Donovan asked.

"Balthazar sent him." Vail said. "He already knows."

Vail ran after the shadow without haste.

"Where are you going?!" Belinda yelled.

"I'm going to see what this spirit knows!" Vail answered. "Don't follow me!"

Belinda went to follow, and Donovan held her back.

"Travis can handle himself."

"That's not what I'm worried about."

Vail chased the shadow, leaving Belinda and Donovan behind. The shadow brought Vail to a spot which was filthy, and the ground was covered in feces and vomit.

"Smells like shit." Vail uttered.

From its appearance, Vail knew it was a spot for homeless people.

"Show yourself, spirit!" Vail yelled.

"In front of him, the shadow appeared. Yet, no fear within it as it morphed into physical form. It resembled a young man, yet he was covered in blood, and chewed on swine's flesh. Vail smirked.

"The hell have we got here. A sin entity."

"Balthazar will have your soul." The entity uttered.

"I think not."

Vail tossed a handful of salt on the entity, startling it. There, Vail began to recite a chant, commanding for the entity to be loosed from Balthazar's hold and to return into the void. The entity was powerful enough to break Vail's chant, forcefully shoving him to the brick wall behind him. Vail fell to the ground and quickly, Kamagrauto arose from the pavement, snatching the entity by the throat and biting it, ripping off its astral head as the body returned to shadow form and fell. Evaporating into thin air.

"I'm not understanding any of this." Vail said.

"You have a higher calling, Travis Vail and I will not allow anyone to turn you away from your cause."

"You know about Balthazar? And how he's behind these plague doctors scaring folks."

"Balthazar has risen up the first sins. Yes. But, there is another spirit lurking the world. One far more powerful than Balthazar and is on the run from another soul as we speak."

"I wish that particular soul the best in his endeavors. Could use the bit of the help every now and then. How come you didn't tell me all this before I went further?"

"I know many things. Things even the smartest man would tremble at the sound."

"Good thing, I'm not the smartest man. I'm just an exorcist."

"One with a higher purpose."

"Then, why don't you just travel onto New York City and stop Balthazar for me? That way, I can focus more on this 'higher purpose'."

'Because it is not my duty to finish your work. You started this case, you must finish it."

Vail chuckled.

"I'll be. You know your kind are some slick sons of bitches."

"Do not compare me to the common demons you've slain."

"I'm not." Vail asked. "But, you really are a strange demon, lad."

"I am not like those demons. I am Kamagrauto. Kamagrauto."

Kamagrauto vanished into the black smoke as before. Vail shrugged himself and scoffed.

V

<u>WHAT CAME ABOUT</u>

Vail returned to Belinda and Galen, who saw his tiredness and often slackly behavior after things have arisen. They approached him with concern and he only smiled.

"What happened to the shadow?" Donovan asked.

"It was taken care of."

"How?" Belinda wondered.

"Kamagrauto killed it."

"The demon Kamagrauto?"

"Yes, Galen. The same demon we met in the alleyway. I confronted the damn thing. By the way, the shadow was a sin entity."

"That can't be so?" Donovan said. "there hasn't been one of them since the World Wars."

"And yet, here it is and not out of curiously either. Balthazar conjured it up."

"What happened to the spirit, Travis?" Belinda asked.

"I nearly came close to casting it away, but it possessed a power that outweigh my voice and tossed me against the wall.

After that, Kamagrauto appeared and decapitated the spirit. Good for me."

"The demon helped you?" Donovan asked. "It killed the spirit right in front of your eyes?"

"Yes. Afterwards we spoke, and he revealed to me he's been aware of this whole case the entire time. I scoffed and wondered how come he couldn't do the work for us. Said it wasn't in his purpose. However, Balthazar is the one behind all of this and there's another sin spirit roaming the earth. But, Kamagrauto confirmed to me that another individual is chasing that spirit right now. So, hopefully we won't have too much work on our hands."

"So, what is our current objective?" Belinda asked.

"Galen, call Colton, tell him to meet us in New York. We need to confront Balthazar now and fast before more of his little ideas manifest into reality."

Vail, Belinda, and Donovan made their travels and arrived in New York City. Prepared to meet Balthazar. Wherever he may reside.

VI

<u>WHAT CAME TO BE</u>

Vail, Belinda, and Donovan stood in Times Square. Seeing the crowds go by, walking about their business. Galen shook his head in shame.

"They're just coming and going."

"It's their nature, Galen. Besides, it proves we're not the ones trapped in Pop Culture and materialism."

"Now, where will Colton be?" Belinda asked.

"He should be around here somewhere."

Vail looked out, not seeing his ally. Later, he turned his head and from there, he managed to get a glance at Colton. He pointed.

"He's coming this way."

Colton Levi approached them and shook hands. Standing in the middle of Times Square mind you amid the roaming crowds.

"Good to see you." Vail said. "Now, why did you want us to meet you out here?"

"Because, the guy you're looking for oftentimes roams through here."

"Are you sure?"

"Plague doctors are seen continually here. It's looked at as just a cosplay show."

"Point us in the direction." Vail said.

They followed Colton through the Square, moving past the crowds. There, Vail and Galen noticed a group of street preachers, yelling at all the white men in the crowds. Vail scoffed as the argument escalated to a brawl.

"They're everywhere."

"It's part of the times, Travis." Donovan said.

"True one."

Colton had led them into a spot where they set shops. He pointed toward the spot which had a crescent moon carved on the door.

"Is this the spot?" Belinda asked.

"It certainly is." Vail confirmed. "Let's see what's inside."

They entered the shop and quickly, surrounded by plague doctors. They raised up their guards as the doctors stood quirt and still.

"Oh, this is the place." Vail said.

The doctors approached them and suddenly, took steps back. Moving in a fashioned line on each side, leading them further into the shop down a hallway. They walked down the hallway and they reached a room. In the room were images of occult symbols, sacrifices, and spells. A pentagram was carved into the wooden floor. Vail stepped forward, seeing a hooded man crouched down at the fire.

"Stand up, you're embarrassing yourself here." Vail said.

The hooded man stood up, removing his hood. Revealing

himself to be Balthazar. Vail smiled. Pointing.

"You son of a bitch!" Vail laughed.

"Travis Vail. The Spirit-Seeker."

"In the flesh."

"I figured you would come."

"Had not choice, lad. I've come to stop your doings. Raising up plague doctors and spirits. The shit has to stop."

"It will not cease until my work is complete."

"Your work is done. Just let it all go. Quit working for the enemy and just retire."

Balthazar raised his hands, shoving Belinda, Galen, and Colton to the floor. Holding them in place with a sort of spiritual bind. Only he and Vail remained standing.

"Why are you doing this?"

"Because I have a master to praise. One who granted me these gifts. I must serve him with all my might."

"Then, your master has to deal with me. And others out there."

"My master's coming was already thwarted by someone. I will not allow the Cryptic Zone to remain shut. He will rise."

"No, he won't."

"And what will you do when he rises and comes for you?"

"Don't all malevolent forces come for me? It's my job to piss your kind off."

"How about a deal."

"A what now?"

"A deal. You leave me to my work and I let your friends live."

"Um, deal declined. However, I can offer you a deal."

"Like so?"

"Let my friends go or find yourself entering Hell a little early than you expected."

"You cannot kill me." Balthazar declared. "No man can murder me!"

"I'm not going to murder you. I'm simply going to offer you a trip. Besides, best you deal with me and not Kamagrauto."

Balthazar froze. His eyes went wider.

"Kamagrauto?" Balthazar asked.

"Yes. You know, lieutenant demon. Works for Dagor the Soul Eater. That kind of guy. He knows of your work by the way. Told me of it. Raising the first sins and all. Plague doctors and such. He knows. And if he knows, who's the say the others know as well."

Balthazar shook, dropping the hold on Belinda, Galen, and Colton. Vail smirked.

"They will not have me." Balthazar said. "My master will protect me!"

"Then, let's see him protect you from this."

Vail raised up his hand, shoving Balthazar down. He began to chant and before he could start, a whirlwind of blue flames surrounded Balthazar. Taking him away. The room was silent. Galen approached the spot. Belinda and Colton were confused.

"The hell just happened?" Colton asked.

"His master took him." Vail said.

"What of the first sins?" Belinda asked. "What of the doctors?"

"We'll see if they still stand." Donovan said.

They returned to the entrance, discovering the doctors are gone. Vail knew Balthazar's fear had driven the doctors and the first sins away. He smirked as they left the shop. The case was done. Yet, Balthazar was somewhere in the world. Possibly in other realms of existence. Vail knew he would see him again down the road.

With everyone returning to their proper places, Vail sat inside his own domain, researching more on the sin entity Kamagrauto mentioned in their conversation. There, Vail discovered there's an ancient power had risen, which is the cause for the sin entity's presence.

"In my line of work, things happen for the worst. Usually the better."

He knew the power was far too great for himself to face. By that standard, Vail went to visit a friend. A friend in Washington D.C.

ABOUT THE AUTHOR

Ty'Ron W. C. Robinson II is the author of several works of fiction.
Including the *Dark Titan Universe Saga*, *The Haunted City Saga*,
EverWar Universe, Symbolum Venatores, Frightened!, Instincts, and
others. More information pertaining to the author and stories can be
found at darktitanentertainment.com.

Twitter: @TyronRobinsonII

Twitter: @DarkTitan_
Instagram: @darktitanentertainment
Facebook: @DarkTitanEnt
Pinterest: @darktitanentertainment
YouTube: Dark Titan Entertainment

www.ingramcontent.com/pod-product-compliance
Lightning Source LLC
Chambersburg PA
CBHW030210130726
47898CB00012B/960